THIS CHANGES EVERYTHING

McLaughlin Brothers, Book 1

JENNIFER ASHLEY

JA / AG Publishing

Chapter One

Zach

"I NOW PRONOUNCE you husband and wife."

About effing time. My oldest brother kisses his true love, and the crowd in the church goes wild.

I'm the best man, at Ryan's side to make sure he can stand up, say his vows, and put the ring on the bride's finger. Then he's Calandra's problem, *her* job to get him back down the aisle and stand still for pictures. I dust off my hands to show Calandra I'm done with him.

By the way, I'm Zach, brother number two. Behind me in the first row are Ben and Austin, both half-sauced and doing victory dances. At least Austin's dancing, punching the air and whooping. Ben's a little quieter, but damn, he's still gyrating around like a big goof.

Why are we partying so hard already? Because we never in our lives thought Ryan McLaughlin and

Calandra Stevenson would get to the altar. It took some doing ...

But hold on a sec. This story isn't about them.

It's about me. And that gorgeous, long-legged sweetheart behind the bride, who can make anything, even a bright yellow butt-ugly maid-of-honor dress, look amazing.

She's got black hair, brown eyes, and curves that can stop traffic. She isn't aware of it—doesn't have her face in the mirror all the time, like women who can't get enough of themselves.

Abby was my first kiss.

Yep. When we were thirteen, she and I mashed lips. I thought I'd die right there. My body was like a river of fire, her lips the softest thing I'd ever felt.

After the seriously wet face smash, we did some staring, our faces red, and started yelling at each other. Ended that relationship real quick.

Hard to believe that was almost twenty years ago. I stayed friends with Abby, more or less, but we never mashed lips again. I didn't care at first because, you know, attention span. Then football ate all my time. It was really, really important, right? More important than watching Abby Warren transform from cute girl to sensuously beautiful woman.

I realized *that* when she showed up to stay with Calandra, her best friend, to get her to the church on time. She's maid of honor to my best man, and we've been thrown together all week.

Yeah, I notice *now*. Not that it's going to do me

any good. I think Abby's with someone or sort of with someone or wants to be with someone, over in Chandler, where she'd moved during high school with her mom when her folks split up. Chandler's like the other side of the planet when you live in north Phoenix.

The music begins to send us back down the aisle. I step away and grin at Ryan, who is so happy it's glowing off him. I swear some of his happiness touches me, like a warm splash in the face. He walks Calandra toward the church's exit, a married man.

Now it's my turn. I hold out my arm and Abby takes it, just like in rehearsal.

Damn, she smells good. The bright yellow dress rustles into my tux as our hips bump.

Her fingers are strong on my arm, warm through the tux jacket. She smiles at me, her lips an orange-red color from whatever lipstick she's wearing.

"They did it," she says to me over the organ music as we skim after my brother and his new wife. "I don't know what I'm going to do now that I don't have to talk Calandra into marrying your brother. A big hole just opened up in my calendar."

"You'll fill it with something. Every time they have a fight ..."

Abby throws me an exasperated glance. "Don't say that. Besides, it's your turn. I had the bachelorette party breakdown. You get their first fight."

I'd heard that Calandra was freaking out a little last night. I got the same from Ryan's end. Ben, Austin, and me had been ready to tie him up and drag him here today.

"I think they'll be fine," I say with confidence. "They just needed to get over the hump."

We study Ryan and Calandra walking out of the church into the sunlight on this April afternoon, leaning into each other. Yep, those two are in love. Humping definitely on their minds.

It starts to be on my mind too. With Abby against my hip, her dark hair dusted with glitter, the faint perfume designed to drive me crazy, how can I help it? She's beautiful. Always has been.

Somehow we get out of the church into the late afternoon sunshine, then it's the endless round of photos, the McLaughlin brothers doing prank poses until Calandra threatens to bean us with her bouquet.

Abby remains poised through it all, far above the rest of us. I get to stand next to her in some pics, and the two of us flank Calandra and Ryan in others. Then the group, with my parents, two people still very much in love.

Calandra and Ryan chose a hiking trip in in northern Arizona for their honeymoon. Whatever floats their boat. I'm betting it isn't so much hiking they have in mind as being alone, far from brothers, parents, and friends.

After photos we zoom off to the resort hotel in north Phoenix we'll all spend the night in. The reception dinner is held in a huge tent outside with a band, food, and plenty of booze. The only flaw is that I have to make a speech.

Abby sits next to me at a long table across the back of the tent, the bride, groom, and wedding party on display. Abby's arms and shoulders are bare, her dress showing a bit of cleavage. Not that I'm looking.

Okay, I'm looking, but I'm keeping my eyes polite. No gaping, gawping, or drooling. I'm a gentleman.

Abby notices my nervousness and puts it down to speech jitters. "Here." She pours her untouched drink into my empty glass. "Courage."

I take a gulp, and cough, my eyes watering. "What is this?"

"Single malt Scotch, no mixer."

"Nice." I venture another sip, savoring this time. "You into whisky?"

Abby shrugs. She has light brown eyes that go well with her dark hair, her irises ringed with gray. I've never seen that in eyes before, and I study them with interest.

"I'm not into tastings and writing stuff in a notebook," she says. "I just like it."

I make a mental note to casually mention Dad's collection of Glenfiddich at some point.

"It's not bad," I say, hefting the glass.

"It's what the bar is serving. Drink it," Abby advises. "Get you over the jitters."

"Or make me so drunk I forget the speech."

She's laughing at me now. "Not if you wrote it down."

"Why would I do that?" I nod at the waiter who's circulating and order Abby another Scotch. "I'm going to wing it."

The corners of Abby's eyes go all crinkly. "Oh, great idea."

"I know. I'm screwed. I don't know what the hell I'm going to say."

The waiter brings the Scotch, which Abby sips. "Don't worry about it. Just say what's in your heart."

"You mean—*I wish I was doing anything but standing up in front of you all making a speech?*"

"You could go with that." Abby nods gravely. "Why don't you? I'd love to see that."

"Heart of gold, that's you."

She laughs. "Well, you suck at kissing, so I want to see if you suck at speeches."

My whole body gets hot, and my face must be red as a brick. "I didn't suck. I was thirteen. What did I know?"

Abby leans closer, and I start getting lightheaded. I shouldn't drink single malt so fast. "Are you saying I was your first kiss?" she asks.

"Yep." I clear my throat. "One I hoped you'd forgotten."

"How could I? It was my first kiss too."

I hadn't known that. I'd gone through puberty thinking I'd made a huge fool of myself with a sophisticated woman. Now I find out, twenty years later, that I worried for nothing.

I raise my glass in salute, and Abby clicks hers

against mine. "In that case," I say, "I think we both sucked."

"There might have been sucking. I'm not really sure."

I lapse into laughter. It had been a stupid moment of my life, and I'm glad she can make fun of it without malice. We'll joke—we'll move on.

Except I suddenly don't want to move on. What has Abby been doing all this time, and what kind of woman has she turned out to be?

A beautiful one with a smattering of freckles on her lightly tanned skin, fascinating eyes, and full-lipped mouth. Plus a hot body, which I am definitely *not* checking out.

My father, Alan McLaughlin, starts tinking his spoon against his glass. The waiters hurriedly finish pouring champagne into flutes and set them down on the tables.

Ryan leans around Calandra to eye me. "You're on, dude."

Shit. I take a gulp of the Scotch and stand up.

"Here's goes nothing," I whisper to Abby, and raise my waiting glass of champagne.

Chapter Two

Abby

ALL ATTENTION TURNS TO ZACH, who can command a room with his blue eyes alone. Dark blue, lined with sexy black lashes that go with his dark hair. The entire family has dark brown hair, ranging from the almost black of Austin's to the red highlights in Ben's. Zach's is in the middle—rich, chocolate, enticing me to run fingers through it.

I haven't seen Zach McLaughlin in years, and I realize I've missed out.

I notice Zach's hand shaking a little—he is *not* happy to speak in public.

Yes, he kissed me when we were middle schoolers, and I went home half-fainting with joy. I figured he'd think me some nerdy girl chasing him if I talked to him again, so I ignored him. The logic of a thirteen-year-old.

We could joke about the kiss now, like old-timers reflecting on days gone by.

Except, I keep wondering what it would be like to kiss him now ...

"Dearly beloved, we are gathered here—" Zach breaks off amid chuckles and his brother Austin's *boo*. "Oh, wait, we already did that. We're celebrating Ryan and Calandra hooking up. *Finally*." More laughter.

Zach waits until his audience is quiet, then he opens his mouth again. And nothing comes out. Maybe a little squeak of air.

He's freezing, with his whole family, their closest friends, and a hundred friends of friends and acquaintances waiting for him to be Mr. Eloquent. I know enough about the McLaughlins, mostly from Calandra talking about them nonstop, to realize they'll never let him hear the end of it if he can't finish his speech.

"Say what's in your heart," I remind him in a hurried whisper.

Zach switches his panicked gaze to me. He is so seriously good-looking I almost lose the thread.

"What?" he asks.

"Say what's in your heart. Go on." I make motions for him to get back to it.

"Sorry." Zach straightens up. "Taking cues from my prompter. The beautiful maid of honor, Abby Warren." He indicates me, and there are *awws* and applause. My face goes hot.

"She's telling me to go with my heart," Zach continues. "So here it is. Ryan, you're a pain in the ass. Now you're Calandra's pain in the ass." A ripple of laughter. "But you know what? It's obvious you two are so much in love. You make each other whole. So be happy Ryan, be happy, Calandra. You know we always have your back, bro. And sis."

More *awws*, even Austin wiping off his grin to applaud. Zach lifts his champagne flute, and the rest of us follow.

"To Ryan and Calandra," he says.

"Ryan and Calandra!" we all shout. Zach sits down, flushed and out of breath.

"How was that?" he says to me under cover of the clapping and cheering.

I take a demure sip of champagne. "Your fly was open."

The horror on his face makes me laugh, my body shaking with it. Zach checks—he has to—finds his pants closed up just fine, and shoots me a vicious glare.

"Oh, you'll pay for that, Abby Warren. You'll pay."

I pretend to myself that his words, his eyes, his voice, don't make my blood run hot. I drink champagne and smile, until his mom comes to hug him and he turns away, giving me a much needed chance to cool down.

———

WEDDING RECEPTIONS PRETTY MUCH FOLLOW THE same pattern unless something goes seriously wrong. I pray as the meal finishes, the sun sets, and dancing begins, that nothing goes wrong. Getting Calandra to the church had been a feat. I deserve seven shots of tequila for pouring her into her dress and driving her there before she could run.

Ryan and Calandra do their first dance. We watch, breathless, as the two gaze into each other's eyes, their love strong.

I relax. They're going to be okay.

The bride and groom finish, and Calandra pairs off with her dad, Ryan with his mom. The rest of the guests stream to the floor to join them. I toss back the last of my champagne from the sidelines and watch, smiling, because my best friend has found happiness.

"Dance?"

Zach is next to me in the shadows beyond the dance floor, his hand out.

He's tall warmth in the dark. His body is hard and honed from whatever workouts he does or whatever sports he engages in. I suddenly want to know which ones.

Should I play it cool? Pretend a shock hasn't gone through me from his nearness, from the enticing way his tux hugs his trim body?

I can try.

"Do you ballroom dance?" I wave my empty champagne flute at the dipping, spinning crowd. "They're waltzing."

"You'd be amazed at what I had to do to prep for this wedding." Zach plucks my glass from my hand and deposits it on the nearest table. "Come on. Need to pay you back, remember?"

"By dancing with me?" I was already swaying to the music. "Not much of a punishment."

His eyes sparkle, and my face scalds. Could I have sounded any more eager?

"By me showing you up on the dance floor," he says.

"You showing *me* up?" I laugh and take his hand, letting him steer me toward the whirling couples. "Oh, honey, it's *on*."

What I haven't told him is I've been practicing. Calandra and I and our friend Brooke signed up for dance lessons in December. We spent the winter and spring learning the waltz, tango, foxtrot, samba, cha cha, and other long-forgotten ways of moving to music.

Zach's been practicing too, I realize as he swings me wide and then tugs me to him, hand landing on my waist in perfect waltz position.

We catch the music, Zach gliding with the three-four time as he spins me around. No tame basic box-step waltz—he's taking me to nineteenth-century Vienna.

I keep up, because, yes, I learned all this. So did Calandra, but a glance shows me she's returned to Ryan and content to cuddle up against him. Zach and I? We're putting it out for all to see.

Austin, the youngest McLaughlin and the show-off, grabs the microphone. "Let's hear it for the *best man* and maid of *honor*. Look at 'em go!"

Everyone is staring now as Zach sweeps me around the floor. We glide-step and spin, sashay back, and glide some more. If I had a train I'd be holding it in a wide arc like a blushing Victorian lady, but I'm in a tame yellow dress, no trains, no whirling skirts.

The music changes, and everyone filters away. The DJ is playing a tango. Where he dug it up, I can't say, but by the sly look on Austin's face, he's slipped the man a twenty to play it.

Not that *he's* tangoing. It's Zach and me. Everyone else edges back to watch, like Zach and I are on a TV dance competition.

Zach takes me along in the slow, quick-quick steps, pushing me with his strong hand on mine, fingers firm on my waist.

The tango is a dance of passion, our instructor told us. The male students had to smolder at their partners, and we ladies had to smolder back. The women were good at it—the guys, horribly embarrassed.

Zach isn't. His eyes hold fire as he gazes deeply into mine. An act, I know, for the dance, but I can't help burning all the way to my toes.

I lift my chin, pretending I'm a sultry lady on a hot night in Buenos Aires. I dare Zach to look away, and he doesn't. A slight flush touches his cheekbones, but other than that, he's in perfect command, no embarrassment.

He tosses me out, and I spin away, brought up short by his strong hand at the fullest extent of my arm. We do our swaying steps, then he twirls me back against him again as everyone applauds.

"They're loving this," I whisper.

"They should. We're awesome." Zach grins. "Want to give them a grand finale?"

"Sure, why not?"

Another spin, and this time I come against him with my back to his front. Nice. I fit well into him, his body curving deliciously over mine.

He twirls me out once more, and we do some good footwork before spinning together again. The music winds toward its conclusion with a sashaying rhythm suggesting warm nights, breathlessness, desire.

Finally Zach pulls me against him, and I end up fully in his arms. He holds my gaze with his, and I read passion in his eyes, which looks good on him, believe me.

Then Zach abruptly dips me, arching me back over his rock-solid arms. A fine place to be. He hangs over me, face a few inches from mine, as I hover above the floor. But I won't fall, I know, because Zach has me.

I play along, gliding my high-heeled shoe up his calf to his thigh. The audience whoops.

Then I realize—Zach *will* drop me. This will be his payback for my crack about his fly.

I brace for it, ready to catch myself as soon as he lets go.

But he doesn't. Zach gently raises me to my feet, sliding his arms from around my waist to take my hand.

The sudden absence of his body heat gives me a cold, empty feeling.

Zach gestures to me with a wave of his hand, and I make a grand bow. He bows with me, and the guests reward us with wild applause.

Austin, who I remember as always loving the spotlight, runs in with a long-stemmed rose from one of the table vases and tells Zach he needs to hold it between his teeth.

Zach snatches the flower from his brother with a scowl, and then turns and presents the rose to me.

"For you, my lady," he says, with an exaggerated bow.

I flutter my lashes. "Why thank you kindly, sir."

The guests think we're hysterical.

Zach leads me from the floor, buoyant. "We should take it on the road."

I plop down in the nearest chair, still clutching the rose. "Once I get my breath. My feet are already killing me."

"Don't move." Zach runs off through the crowd.

More music begins, this time modern stuff, which doesn't require months of lessons. You go in, shake your groove thing, and have fun.

Zach returns with two tall glasses of ice water. I gulp mine with relief. It's April in Phoenix, and it was in the nineties today, only about eight-five now. We're dancing in an outdoor tent like it's nothing, because we like to sweat.

I down the water and a waiter appears bearing two

drinks that look like piña coladas. "I thought we deserved it after that show," Zach says, taking the glasses and thanking the waiter.

He sits down and lifts his glass of frothy white ice in a toast. "To dirty dancing."

"Wasn't dirty." I click my piña against his and take a sip. Cool coconut and pineapple slide over my tongue, quenching my thirst. The bite of rum doesn't hurt either. "That was classic ballroom dancing."

"Hot stuff, back in the day." Zach winks at me, his cute blue eyes drawing me in.

He'd had the same effect when I'd been a gawky kid, falling in love for the first time. Or what I thought was love. A huge crush, I realize now, pure and simple. Not that I blame the girl I was for the crush.

"Isn't this kind of a sissy drink for you?" I hold up my glass, half empty. "Shouldn't you be throwing back more shots of single malt?"

"Who cares? A drink's a drink. As long as it's good." Zach takes a gulp. "And this one's good. Talented bartender. Only the best for Ryan."

He says it without resentment, as though he approves.

We drink a bit more, a silence descending. I wouldn't mind simply sitting here basking in Zach, enjoying the view, but I also fear he'll finish his drink and walk away.

I mean, we're nothing to each other. We've come together tonight to celebrate my best friend and his brother finally joining at the altar. We shared a dance to take the pressure off Calandra and Ryan, to let them have a moment while Zach and I commanded the attention.

What is left?

"So ..." is my scintillating conversation opener. "What have you been up to since, oh, eighth grade?"

Zach laughs, gravelly and sexy. He doesn't have a model-perfect face, too hard for pin-up photos, but he still manages to be gorgeous. There's character in that face, eyes that have gazed upon the world and decided how he'd be in its context.

"Let's see." Zach watches the dancers, thoughtful. "Played a lot of football. Finished high school. Went to college. Started working for my folks. That's pretty much it." Again, no resentment. I hear no regrets about his life.

"You were really good at football, I heard." I poke at what's left of the drink with my straw. "Did you continue in college?"

"Nah. I loved playing, but I wasn't great, you know? Not the kind of devote-your-whole-damn-life to being an expert at catching a ball kind of great. I didn't want to make something I enjoyed into work, know what I mean?" Zach breaks off and gives a self-deprecating laugh. "My way of saying I didn't make it past tryouts. But I really didn't care. I remember wondering why I was so relieved when I didn't make the team, not even second string. It helped me realize there were other things to be interested in. So now I play with my brothers and friends for fun." Zach tosses back the rest of his drink. "Your turn."

My face heats. "Nuh-uh," I say quickly. "You're not done. That was just the explanation of why you didn't play football in college. What else happened to you?"

He shakes his head. "This is me trying not to make my life boring. I finished college and started working for my mom and dad at their business. End of story."

"No, no, no." I wave my glass. The waiter, taking it as a signal, brings us two more. "Not end of story. Did you fall in love? Meet someone? She's not here, so either she's not feeling well or doesn't want to have anything to do with weddings. Or *he*, if that's the case."

Zach's laughing at me the whole time but I note a flicker of pain in his eyes. "No *he*. Or *she*. I'm not in a relationship."

I swirl my second piña. "See, this is the difference between men and women. If you were a woman, I'd already know every detail about why you aren't with whoever it was. Who was she, and what happened?"

"You're right. A guy friend would say, *Women, what can you do?*, smack me on the shoulder, and order me another drink."

"You haven't finished that one." I point at the half-empty glass in his hand. "Spill the beans. I won't post it on social media. Cross my heart."

Zach's smile dims. "Why do you want to know so bad?"

"I want to know everything about you, Zach McLaughlin." The piña coladas are catching up to me, not to mention the Scotch and the champagne I had before the dance. I'm talking far more freely than I would otherwise. "Everything I missed by moving away from the old neighborhood."

"I asked her to marry me." Zach's affability fades. "She laughed and said no way was she marrying anyone. Two months later, she runs off with my best friend—my *ex*-best friend—to Las Vegas where they got married by Elvis."

He finishes, clamps his mouth shut, and gulps down his piña colada.

Chapter Three

Zach

DAMN IT, I don't want to talk about it. Haven't since it had happened two years ago. A woman and I guy I'd trusted with my life had ground rocks into my face and walked away.

I don't want to talk about it to beautiful Abby Warren, gazing at me with sympathy in her big brown eyes.

She straightens up. Signals to the waiter. "Does he have any whisky over there? Good stuff?"

The waiter, a young kid probably just thrilled he gets to carry drinks around to drunk wedding partiers, says he'll check and scuttles away.

"It was a long time ago," I say. "I'm over it."

"Don't lie to me." Abby leans in. "I was your first, remember?"

The glitter in her hair catches the light. It had

sparkled and gleamed while we danced, she laughing at me with her coral-lipsticked mouth. The lipstick is a little smeared now, left on the glasses she's drunk from, but it doesn't detract from her at all. Her natural lip color shows through, red and sexy.

"You still remember that awful kiss," I say, my face warm.

"You remember it too," she accuses me. "Or you wouldn't know it was awful."

"I didn't know what I was doing." The young waiter brings over two glasses of amber liquid, neat. I reach into my pocket and toss a twenty onto his tray. "That's for you."

The kid stares at it. "Oh, I'm not supposed to accept tips tonight."

"Don't tell anyone," I whisper.

He looks me fully in the eye for the first time then grins and says thanks. The twenty vanishes and the kid walks off with a spring in his step.

"Nice of you." Abby is happy with me.

"Probably is getting a crap wage from the hotel for working his ass off." I shrug, lift the whisky. "Here's to … a great dance."

Abby clicks her thick glass to mine. "Nah. Here's to you dodging a bullet."

I blink, glance around the tent. "What bullet? What are you talking about?"

"I mean your girlfriend. First of all, any woman who walked out on you must be an idiot. You want to be tied to an idiot? Second, she was obviously sizing up your best friend at the same time, and he was ... what's that called? ... bird-dogging. Obviously neither of them gave a shit about you. And seriously, they were married by a cheesy Elvis impersonator and thought it romantic? You should be thanking your lucky stars you found out about them before they mired you in their drama and bogged down your entire life. It's like you finding out you wanted to play football for fun, not make it into work."

She speaks emphatically, close enough to me that I can breathe her perfume, watch the sparkles in her hair. She punctuates her words with her jabbing fingers. They aren't sharp claws—she has real nails, neatly trimmed and touched with pink polish.

Abby finishes delivering her speech and lifts her whisky. "So, here's to you. For being a bad-ass. Free of people who have no brains or compassion."

"When you put it that way." I raise my glass. "I *am* pretty bad-ass, aren't I?"

"Damn straight."

We click glasses and down the whisky. I get up and go for more.

I half expect her to be gone when I return, or dancing with a guy who can't get enough of her. But Abby's there, watching the crowd bounce up and down to the music, her feet tapping to the beat.

A lady who likes to dance. I picture us in clubs, in the dark, dancing side by side, laughing, or holding each other close.

I push aside the thought. I'm lonely, I'm half drunk,

she's beautiful, and I have a connection to her, if an awkward one, from childhood. I remind myself we're here to celebrate a wedding, and that's it.

Abby smiles at me as I hand her the whisky, and my reasoning goes to hell. She's lovely, she's funny, and after tonight, it might be a long time before I see her again, if ever. You get swallowed into your routine, and you rarely leave your circle, even with the best intentions.

"Enough about me," I say, sitting next to her. "What about you? How's your life treating you?"

Abby takes the glass I hand her, our fingertips brushing. "Oh, you know. You get through it."

"Let me be nosy now. What have you been up to in the last twenty years?"

Abby laughs, her eyes softening. "Pretty much same as you. High school, college. I moved to Chandler because my parents split up, which you probably know. Lived with my mom—we took care of each other. I always envied you with your big family."

She sounds wistful. I've done my share of complaining about my interfering brothers, and have yelled more than once that I wished I were an only child, but I know I'm lucky. I have three best friends, and because they're my brothers, if I tell them to get lost for a while, I'm reasonably sure they'll be around when I'm not as crabby. Same in reverse when they're sick of me.

"I can't deny it's been good," I say.

Abby perks up, as though she can't stay down long.

"My mom and I were good together too—no huge dramas. She got married a few years ago to a guy who's been around a long time. Jim. He's always been like a dad to me."

Abby appears happy about this, so I figure things turned out for the best.

"You and your brothers work in the same business?" she asks in admiration. "Calandra told me a little bit, but not much—when she talks about Ryan it's how good-looking he is, and how sweet, and how well he skis, among other things ..." She flushes, and I hold up my hands.

"I do not want to know those other things about my brother."

"I didn't want to know them either." Abby's shuddering with me. "I'm amazed you have a family business in this day and age."

"It's more common than you think," I say. "We're renovators, sort of. When you move into a house, even a new build, and it's crap, we come in and replace the junk with decent stuff—appliances, windows, doors, cabinets, whatever. We also work with developers when they're building in the first place, so the stuff inside the house is better quality." I screw up my face. "And now I sound like our brochure. Please shut me up." I drink my whisky in desperation.

"No, it's cool. I work in a giant corporation on a massive campus—I'm lucky I can find my way to my cubicle. The small business sounds nice."

"Lots of work, but we do it. Ryan's the heir apparent." I gesture with my glass to my brother who is holding his bride, a dazed look on his face. "He works closest with my dad and mom to keep us running. He'll take over when they retire." I have no envy about that—better him than me, is my thought. "Ryan is the best bro a bro can have. Ben's our IT guy." I point out Ben, two years younger than me. He's been cornered by Dad's aunt Mary, and is nodding politely at her—he's nice like that. "A total geek, but what Ben can't do with a computer program isn't worth knowing. Austin is the screw-up." Austin, the youngest, is dancing with a sleek young woman in a slinky gown— figures. "He's a good salesman, though. Knows the business and can bring us clients like it's nothing. Doesn't break a sweat and is surprised when we mention his talents."

"And your mom?" Abby glances at my parents, Virginia and Alan, who are surrounded by friends, so happy their firstborn has married a fine young woman. Their words.

"Mom runs all the financials," I explain. "Without her, we'd be toast. She's Mrs. Numbers. Ben takes after her."

Abby pins me with her bewitching gaze. "What about you? Are you management, computer geek, or brilliant salesman masquerading as a screw-up?"

I shrug. "None of those. I take up the slack on what everyone's too busy for. I keep track of our charitable work, or I'll land a client Austin's found, or make sure Ben has the hardware he needs—half the time, I have no idea what the hell Ben's talking about, but I know where to order it."

"Ah." She's impressed, to my surprise. "You're the linchpin."

"I think of it as batting cleanup. You know—if they're too busy or it's out of their sphere ... call in Zach."

"And you ballroom dance the clients into submission?" Her nose wrinkles with her smile. It's adorable.

"Yeah, that's one part of it." I give her a wise look. "You'd be amazed how often it comes up."

"I've seen your ads around town," Abby says. "McLaughlin Renovations. Very functional."

"It gets the point across. We hired a PR firm once to spread the word, but it cost more than it really helped. I about shit myself when I saw Austin's face on the side of a bus. I was glad when that ad ended. I was scared to drive anywhere for a while." I feign a shudder.

Abby chuckles and sips her whisky. "Poor Zach. I asked because that's what I do—sales."

"Oh yeah?" I lift my brows. "Do you stroke the merchandise and make it look sexy?"

I'd never have said that if I wasn't mostly drunk. And she wasn't so sexy. Would she throw the drink in my face and walk off?

No, she laughs again. Whew.

"I wish," Abby says. "Selling what my company makes is harder than you think. I have to explain whatever gadget the hot new thing is and why people need it. I don't always understand what it does myself. I sit in booths at trade fairs and say, *We have the latest doo-dad that will increase your productivity ten-thousand percent. Would you like a pen?"*

She holds out the rose in demonstration. I take it.

"Why thank you, ma'am," I drawl. "I'll order a dozen boxes of your doodads, no problem." I'd take anything Abby offered me.

"Aren't you sweet? Most people stare at me blankly and walk away, or they explain why *their* company's doodad is so much better than ours."

"Ungrateful bastards."

"I always say that."

"Out loud?"

"Depends." Abby smiles so wickedly that I want to hold her as close as I had in the tango.

I lay down the rose and stick out my hand. "Want to dance some more? You can barely sit still. Either that or you need the bathroom."

"Hilarious. Let's go"

"To the bathroom?"

Abby grabs my hand as she stands up. "If you want. I'm going to *dance*, my friend."

And we do. We find the rhythm and shake it— damn, can she shake it. My eyes stay on Abby's curvy figure, legs that know how to move.

We join hands and do some ballroom dancing to the tunes, for the hell of it. People applaud us. Ryan and Calandra don't notice—but they don't need to. They're lost in their own world, as they should be.

Austin dances up and tries to take Abby away from

me, but she, the sweetheart, waves him off. Austin points two fingers at me like, *You rock, dude,* and gyrates away. Ben's now dancing with Great Aunt Mary. If I was noble, I'd rescue him, but I have Abby, and Great Aunt Mary is making some good moves.

In the glare of the string lights, with my friends and family dancing like fools around me, Abby is a glow in the grayness. My life isn't terrible, but there's not much to it either—day by day fixing problems and helping my parents, hanging out with the brother pack or friends, most nights on my own.

Ryan's starting his own life now, and it won't be the same. I'm happy for him, but he'll be missing in the four-pack. That fact and all the drinking is making me a little sad.

But sadness vanishes when I focus on Abby. Beautiful woman, warm night, hot music. I want more.

Will I have more? That's a speculation I can't answer. Whatever Abby's thinking, she keeps to herself as she dances like a goddess in yellow, a firefly in the dark.

————

THE CROWD IS WELL RELAXED WHEN RYAN AND Calandra, who'd disappeared for a while, reappear dressed for their drive up to the mountains. They've decided not to spend the night in the hotel—wise. Ryan doesn't trust us, his three brothers, to leave them alone. Even Ben would join in the practical jokes.

Calandra's mom is hugging her, tears in her eyes. Her dad, the same. Shaking Ryan's hand, as if to say, *Take good care of her, son.*

Ryan would. Mr. Stevenson didn't have to worry. The rest of us would take care of Calandra too. She was family now.

Damned if my eyes aren't wet. Abby and I must have drunk a *lot*.

Calandra's ready to throw her bouquet. In the movies, women mob each other to catch it, but the ladies here look almost afraid of it. I don't know if they're being nonchalant or in no rush to tie themselves to some guy who can't wash his own clothes.

Calandra turns her back, Ryan sidestepping out of the way. She tosses.

The bouquet goes up and up—a long, spinning pass. She's got a good arm, even backwards. Abby watches, bemused, as the bunch of flowers, ribbons fluttering, hits its arc and comes down, down, down ...

Straight into the arms of my little brother Ben.

We shout with laughter. Bright red, Ben quickly shoves the bouquet at Great Aunt Mary. She takes it in delight.

"Why thank you, sweetie." Great Aunt Mary wears a redder lipstick than Abby's, her silver hair perfectly coiffed. "Wouldn't mind a little of that action."

We laugh again, Great Aunt Mary taking the pressure off Ben. It's why she's everyone's favorite.

Ryan and Calandra depart amid hugs, well wishes, and waves.

The DJ continues with the music as Calandra and Ryan vanish into the darkness, but the heart has gone out of the party. People begin drifting away, heading for the hotel rooms booked for the wedding party and guests.

"I guess it's over." Abby sorrowfully glances around the emptying dance floor.

"We could go on to a club, if you want."

She shakes her head, shoulders slumping. "It was more fun with friends and family. Clubs can be ... impersonal."

True. If you aren't with a group of friends, clubs can be boring as hell. I grope around in my mind, trying to come up with a way we can hang out together longer. The number of places in Phoenix open after nine p.m., even on a Saturday night, are few and far between.

I open my mouth to suggest the bar here at the hotel, when Abby says, "Walk me to my room?"

As I stare, my mouth frozen in its open position, Abby flushes. "I'm a little drunk," she says hurriedly. "I don't want to be found face-down in the hall in the morning."

"Sure." I'm a gallant gentleman. Of course I'll escort a lady home.

I offer my arm, and she takes it. We're both unsteady, and she leans into me, soft woman against my side.

No one comments on us leaving. Most of the guests are gone anyway, except Ben. I feel his eyes on my back, but Ben I trust. He's not one to gossip and ruin a lady's rep.

The hotel is a swank one, with many wings surrounding the grounds—giant pool, open air patio, perfect for our winter weather, beautiful on a mild April night.

Abby's on the second floor, in a suite. Apparently they dressed the bride there.

We take the elevator, too shaky to walk up a flight of stairs, and find her door. Abby fishes her key from a tiny pocket in her dress, a pocket that would never fit more than a key card. She starts to hover the card over the reader, and hesitates.

"Want to come in?" she asks in a shy voice.

Do I? Shit, yeah. Heat rocks my body, though she's only asked me to go inside. Maybe to help her clean up from the bridal outfitting. I picture female accoutrements everywhere—gloves, hats, ribbons, whatever women wear to weddings these days. Maybe even embarrassing pieces of underwear.

Then again, Abby's smile doesn't tell me she's interested in a little housecleaning.

I swallow. "Sure," I try to say casually. The word is a hoarse grunt. "Why not?"

I take the key from her and wave it over the pad. Fortunately, the light turns green on the first try, so I don't have to make several clumsy attempts.

The lock clicks. I shove the door all the way open, gesturing Abby inside. "After you, my lady."

Chapter Four

Abby

THERE'S a bottle of blood-red wine in the front room, courtesy of Calandra and Ryan. I guess Calandra figured I'd need it after wrestling her to her own wedding. I wonder if there's one in Zach's room.

The bridesmaids and I had packed up Calandra's stuff before going down to see her married, and she'd taken the suitcases when she left with Ryan. This room is tidy, my things hidden away in the bedroom.

I kick off my shoes, happy to be out of the heels. I offer the wine—we've danced so much my buzz has worn off a little. Zach, a gentleman, opens it and pours.

"To success," he says to me, and we touch glasses before we drink.

I know he means the wedding and us making it through to the end. Ryan and Calandra are off to the mountains, and we can relax.

"I'll miss her," I say with sudden sadness as I sit down.

"Yeah, I know what you mean." Zach stretches out in a chair and crosses his feet. "Ryan's a pain in the ass, but he's a good brother. I'll be glad when he comes home."

"They need some time alone, those two kids." I try to keep my voice light.

"Serious time alone. What about you?" Zach skewers me with his baby blues. "Who do you spend alone time with?"

"My dog."

"Yeah? What kind of dog?"

"German Shepherd. Mixed with ... something. He's a rescue. He's my mom's dog actually, but I love the guy." Muttly is a sweetheart and better company than a lot of men I've known.

"I have a big yard but no pets at the moment." Zach sounds regretful, which makes me believe he likes dogs. A plus.

"I know you want to ask if I have a boyfriend," I say. "The answer is nope. I was going out with a guy, but it fizzled."

It fizzled because I couldn't talk to him. I mean, not even normal day-to-day conversation, let alone anything deep. I'd start on a topic, and he'd brush it off. Or I'd say, "I ran into—*name of mutual acquaintance*—today ..." and he'd say scornfully, "So?"

It became obvious he didn't give a shit about me or

who I talked to, or anything I did or wanted to do, so I stopped calling him, and he stopped calling me.

I find myself telling Zach all this. He listens. Not pretends to listen while drinking his wine, checking his texts, scrolling through his social media, wondering what's on the sports channels ... He listens. Looks at me. Not through me.

I don't sob about the guy I drifted apart from. I simply tell the story, and Zach nods as though he understands.

The conversation continues. Zach and I talk about so many things—people we used to know from our old school, what our parents are up to, what we're doing now.

"So why do you still live in Chandler?" he asks as the wine bottle slowly empties.

I take a sip and shrug. "It's close to work, close to my mom, has easy access to the lakes and mountain hiking. What's not to love? Why do you live in mid-town Phoenix?" I counter.

His lips twitch. "Close to work, has cool historic houses, access to hiking, close to sports venues. Plenty to love. Except the traffic."

I roll my eyes. We talk about traffic, because everyone in Phoenix does, and about how long it takes to get anywhere, and why the hell is there always so much construction?

We turn to the things we want to do in our lives— both of us have an itch to travel. He wants to hike the

Arizona Trail, which stretches from one end of the state to the other. I think that would be cool. I'd like to go up north—by which I mean the Arizona Strip, north of the Colorado River, and to the Vermillion Cliffs. Zach stops short of asking if we should go together, and so do I.

I like this bubble of casualness—no pressure, no anticipation, no practicalities. Just friends catching up on old times, talking about what we might do, what we dream of doing, no expectations that we have to do anything at all.

Soon I have my feet curled up, wondering if I dare duck into the other room and take off my bra. He unties his bow tie and opens his coat but doesn't take the coat off, like he's comfortable. I don't want to leave the room, because he might not be here when I come back.

We get started on the differences between a man's take on weddings and a woman's. I'm surprised Zach doesn't think all women get weepy about white ribbons and tulle, and he laughs at me when I say bachelor parties are about strippers and sports.

"We drank beer, cooked out, and shot the breeze." Zach lounges farther down into his chair, legs outstretched. "Talked about old times and made fun of Ryan. Made fun of him a lot. Austin wanted a stripper, but Ryan said no. His party, his rules." Zach sends me a sly glance. "I hear you ladies had one, though."

I flush. "Maybe." Yes, we did. We truly did. That was one hot man falling out of a Velcro-ed suit.

Not as hot as Zach, some demon inside me whispers.

"What did he dress up as?" Zach asks. "Fireman? Cop? Botanist?"

I chuckle. "Stripper. He wore a tux, actually. Pretended to be the best man ..." I trail, off my face flaming, as the best man in front of me collapses into laughter.

"Seriously?" he splutters.

"His choice. We didn't rehearse him."

Zach jumps to his feet. Sways to his feet more like. The wine bottle is all but finished.

"Something like this?" He sidles his shoulders, peeling his coat from them and catching the coat with his arms.

"Stop." I hold out my hand, unable to contain my laughter. Also, his mimicry is making me horny. Zach is a fine-looking man.

Zach lets the coat slide from his arms to the floor. He starts scatting "The Stripper" in a raunchy voice. *"Dah dah dant dant, dah dah dant dant ..."*

Off comes his cummerbund, which flies across the room. He's wearing suspenders, which he stretches out comically before he drops them down his shoulders. Zach streams the dangling bow tie from around his neck like a feather boa and emphatically throws it to the floor.

Now he's unbuttoning his shirt. *Pop, pop, pop* go the buttons, his throat and chest bared by the V in his undershirt coming into view.

I'm on my feet, dancing to his singing. I must be drunk, because I start unzipping the back of my dress.

Whew, it's a relief to loosen it. I unhook my bra, exhaling for the first time all night.

Zach keeps on with the shirt, grinning at me, encouraging. He thrusts the shirt down his arms. There's a funny moment when the cuffs get caught on his wrists, but he determinedly wrenches them open, buttons flying, as he keeps up the song.

I sing along. I'm not really going to strip, says the back of my mind, even as I slip my arms out of the cap sleeves. I hold the dress to my bosom and shimmy out of my stockings. It's way too hot for those.

The two of us dancing around pretend stripping brings us close. I fling my stockings aside and ram right into him.

Everything stops.

The room grows silent, the music in my head puttering out.

Zach's face is near mine. His beard shadow has deepened in the last hours, lamplight burnishing it. He looks straight into my eyes, as though he can see everything inside me, everything lonely, everything sad, every missed opportunity.

In him I read the same loneliness, the feeling of standing on the sidelines of life. Tonight we're standing there together.

To hell with it. I slam myself against him and kiss him full on the mouth.

Electrifying. I'm not kidding. A jolt runs down my body and out my feet as I wrap my arms around him.

A long time ago, on a planet far, far away, Zach

kissed me. We were thirteen, me wondering what it would be like to kiss a boy.

I'd been both floored and disappointed. The touch of warmth, the intimacy, knocked me back, but the wet inexperience had made me decide it had been a bad idea.

Twenty years later, kissing Zach McLaughlin is a completely different story.

Warmth and intimacy flood me again, but our inexperience has vanished. Zach's lips are firm, his kiss full of heat. He cups the back of my neck and pulls me closer, tongue opening my mouth.

I welcome him in, tasting the wine, the whisky, the spice that is Zach. That spice excites me, makes me want more. The kiss turns fierce, and I have a burning in my bones that tells me where this is going.

After a long time, Zach slides his hands to my shoulders, encouraging my loosened dress down my arms. Next he catches the straps of my bra, which fall after my dress.

His hands find my breasts, his palms hard with outdoor work, but gentle, caressing. Zach's kisses also caress, and our lips meet in silence, our bodies close as we explore each other.

Zach releases me from the kiss, drawing a ragged breath as he gazes at me. "The beauty of you," he whispers. "It's blowing me away."

I flush, loving the compliment and not knowing what to do with it. For answer I push open his shirt, running my hands across his T-shirted chest. I feel his heart beating beneath my fingertips, pound-pounding as his ribcage rises with his breath.

I tug at the T-shirt, wanting him as bare as I am.

Zach grins and pulls the shirt off over his head. I feast my eyes on the dense muscles of his torso, his six-pack abs that attest to a lot of crunches at the gym.

The smooth skin of his chest is dusted with black hair, wiry curls catching my fingertips. His flat nipples tighten under my touch.

Zach makes a noise in his throat. His thumb caresses the tips of my nipples, the fire he starts making me incoherent. I tilt my head for more kisses, needing them, desire hot between my legs.

He holds me with one hand planted solidly on my back, the other lightly on my breast while he kisses me. And kisses me. I wriggle my fingers under his waistband, reaching for the honed ass I'd spied inside his tux trousers.

I find the satin skin, the tight flesh. Another noise leaves his throat as I let my fingers play.

Zach breaks off, breathless, eyes heavy as he looks down at me. "Abby ..."

The name caresses me as much as his fingers on my bare skin.

"Let's take this to the bedroom," I whisper.

Here's his chance to run, to find his brothers and laugh about how easy his childhood flame, Abby Warren, has become.

Zach gazes down at me with need. "Okay."

I take his hand, and lead him there.

Zach

ABBY APOLOGIZES FOR THE MESS IN THE BEDROOM of her suite, but I barely notice the boxes, the makeup on top of the dresser, the silk flowers piled next to the television. I glimpse Calandra's bridal gown hanging in the closet before Abby swiftly closes its door.

She comes to me, holding the yellow fabric of her bridesmaid's dress over her fabulous breasts. She has curves, does Abby. I can't wait to touch them again.

The bed is smooth and inviting, the pillows plumped, sheets turned down for the night. There's a chocolate on each nightstand. This hotel is big on service.

I can't believe Abby's inviting me to stay, but I'm not arguing either. She gives me her lopsided smile, her eyes sparkling as we approach the bed.

I want to kiss her again, so I pull her into my arms. Her mouth tastes of sweetness and smooth wine, her lips plump. I gently bite her lower one.

Her dress falls as she lifts her arms to encircle my neck, and I help it shimmy all the way to the floor. She'd already tossed off her stockings in the other room, so I have a nearly naked Abby against me, except for the tiny slash of her yellow underwear, which matches the dress.

I'm so busy enjoying kissing and touching her that I don't realize she's undone my pants until they're around my ankles. That must be so sexy—a guy with his pants pooling around his socks and shoes.

The trousers are loose, so I kick them away.

Abby pulls back to look me over. The smile she beams tells me she's laughing her ass off at me, but I don't care. The sight of her, bare for me, tan lines around her shoulders and waist, more than make up for me looking stupid.

I take advantage of the lull to toe off my shoes. I try pulling off my socks, but they get stuck, and I'm hopping, tugging at the black torture devices. Meanwhile Abby's laughing some more.

She disappears into the bathroom, and for a second, I fear she's going to shut and lock the door, leaving me to gather up my clothes and slither off, but she's out almost right away, dropping something on the nightstand. I don't see what it is as I'm now on the edge of the bed, yanking off the socks.

Abby stands before me, five foot five of beautiful. Hands on my shoulders, she slowly pushes me back onto the bed.

I let her. I surrender. Why the hell wouldn't I?

Right in front of me my eyes, she peels off her underwear and then leans to me, fingers tugging at my waistband.

I wriggle out of the boxer briefs and send them after my socks. My cock is standing up straight, impressed with Abby. Wanting her. Excitement pumps through me like a shot of single malt.

She gazes at my cock and then reaches out and runs

her fingertips up it.

I almost explode. I seize her by the arms and pull her down to the bed, kissing her, wanting to be inside her more than I've ever wanted anything in my life.

The bed shakes as I turn her on her back, coming down on top of her. She's a warm armful, squirming against me without coyness. Her eyes hold me, the soft brown shining as much as the glitter in her hair.

Abby flutters one hand to the nightstand, and I see it. Condom. Wow, this hotel is truly prepared ...

I snatch it up. "Where did this come from?"

"Calandra." Abby's face turns scarlet. "She gave me a box as a joke."

"Ha ha," I say, deadpan. "Funny. And convenient."

"Because she knows you were my first kiss, and she said when we got together again, sparks would fly."

I consider this for about two seconds, maybe less. "Don't care. Thank you, Calandra," I say to the air.

I rip open the packet and drop to the bed to slide the thing on. It's cold, and I don't like condoms, but they're necessities if you're going to have a one-night-stand.

I hesitate another split second. Is that what this is? What it will be? A one-night-stand with Abby and nothing more?

My body is on fire, my adrenaline off the scale. *Worry about it later.*

Abby welcomes me down to her, her smile as sweet as a summer day. I brush back her hair, kiss her mouth, and slowly slide inside her.

Chapter Five

Abby

IS this what happiness feels like? Zach, my old friend, my first glimpse of what passion might be, looks into my eyes with his amazing blue ones, and presses himself into me.

I groan with it. I can't stop myself. His warm weight sends me into softness, and his hardness touches something inside me I don't think I've ever experienced. I've had lovers before, but the instant Zach connects with me, it's like a bell sounding, a completion of something I've been waiting for all my life.

He goes very still, his eyes intense. He's filling me, stretching me. I reach for his hips, those tight muscles welcoming my hands. I cradle him, pulling him farther in.

Zach leans down and kisses me, mouth hot, and

then he glides out and back in again, starting a rhythm that is the best thing in the world.

I lift myself to him. When we'd tangoed, I'd laced my foot around his leg, and I do it again. This is what the tango is about. Wild passion that's the closest thing to sex you can do in front of other people.

"Abby." Zach's throaty groan spirals heat into me. "I've never ..."

What he's never done gets lost as he closes his eyes and pumps, our bodies crashing together, held in the best kind of dance.

"Zach." I touch his face, his shoulder, return to squeezing his seriously fine ass. "Damn."

"Exactly." Zach slides in and out, the mattress groans, and I swear the pictures on the walls shake.

The pillows slide out from under my head and I slap them away. Easier to push myself up to him on a flat mattress, and I want more and more and more. Zach slides his hand between us, his thumb bringing me to life as he presses deep inside.

Dark waves of ecstasy pour down to sweep me away. I hear the screams from my mouth, the cries of need, the words I never say at work. Zach's laughing, but in sheer pleasure, then his laughter dies and his face scrunches up.

"Shit!" The word is a whisper and a groan. Zach's head goes back, lamplight glistening on his skin as he grows louder. "*Shit!*"

He drives inside me as I try to hold him tighter than I possibly can. Zach lets out another strangled sound, and then he's coming too, pounding the bed with one fist as he releases.

We both gasp for breath as he collapses to me, kissing my face and hair, saying my name as though he loves me.

It must be wonderful to be loved by Zach ...

I hold him close, kissing his lips, wishing this night will never end.

———

Zach

I WAKE UP KNOWING SOMETHING IS SERIOUSLY right with the world. I drowse for a few minutes, wondering why I feel so good. Warm, comfortable, happy.

Then I remember.

I open my eyes in panic. Will Abby be gone? Did she take her luggage and run? Leaving me to hobble back to my room, hungover, unwashed, doing the walk of shame?

I turn my head ... and there she is. The most beautiful woman in the world, gazing back at me.

She flushes a pretty red. "Morning."

"Morning."

Silence. We stare at each other a few moments, as though neither of us wants to break the magic. Real life is out there, but it's far away. The routine of showers, breakfast, checking the news, checking email, dealing with work problems ... it's hovering, remote, not a part of this place and time.

The relief she's still here smacks me hard. Abby shows no shock that we actually slept together or that she wants any excuse to get away from me.

We keep looking at each other, each waiting for the other to start. Or stop.

Abby touches my cheek. I feel her tickle my unshaved whiskers as though she likes them.

"What do we do now?" she asks softly.

My cock is already hard and waiting. "I know what I want to do."

A tiny smile, hope. "What's that?"

"Brush my teeth." I slide my hand over my mouth. It can't be good, my breath, not after a night of whisky, champagne, piña coladas, wine and all the yelling I did while having sex.

Her smile deepens. "No problem. There's an extra toothbrush in the bathroom, in my toiletries bag. In the package, I mean. Never used."

I flood with happiness, because I won't have to leave her yet, then my eyes narrow. "Wait, why did you bring an extra toothbrush?"

"In case I drop mine in the toilet." Abby shrugs. "It happens. Hotel bathrooms can be tricky."

I burst out laughing. In time, I remember to turn my head and not blast her with morning breath. "Be right back."

I roll out of bed, my feet bouncing on the floor. I

feel light, effervescent, which I shouldn't. I should be hung over and sick. Why aren't I?

Because I had the best sex of my life last night, that's why. The rush of it probably burned out all the alcohol.

Abby wolf whistles. I turn around. "What?"

"You have a great ass, McLaughlin. You know that?"

"Aw." I shake it for her. "Nothing compared to yours."

Abby props herself on her elbow. "Have you been checking out my ass?"

"Yep. If you can ogle me, I'm doing it right back."

"Okay." Abby gives me a slow once over, making my body hotter than my back yard in July.

I hate to leave her, but I really want to meet that toothbrush.

I find it in her toiletries bag—with compartments and everything tidy, unlike my just-throw-it-in jumble. By the time I have the toothbrush out, coated with toothpaste and in my mouth, Abby is with me, doing the same thing.

I never thought brushing teeth would be sexy. But it is. Naked, side-by-side, the mirror reflecting two people with messed up hair, brushing furiously. Abby's breasts move, and I get lost watching them.

I have a sudden thought—what would it be like to be with her every day? Go through the whole deal— shower, emails, dealing with problems, coming home to talk about everything with Abby?

I have never in my life pictured this. Now it slams me in the face like a cream pie in a slapstick routine.

I freeze, stunned, but the vision doesn't go away. Abby continues brushing then rinses her mouth and hangs up the toothbrush. She gives me a puzzled glance, wondering why the hell I'm standing there with the toothbrush sticking out of my mouth.

I quickly finish up, rinse and spit, taking the towel she offers me.

Before she can ask what I want to do next, I throw the towel to the counter, slide another condom out of the box, put my arm around her, and take her back to bed. The sheets are still warm, the perfect nest for me to lower her into before I lick her all over. I do mean all over. Every inch. Some inches I linger on more than others.

Then she does me. Her tongue drives me insane. What she can do with her mouth ... holy *fuck*.

I can't take it. I roll on the condom in record time then wrap myself around her and make love to her, hard and fast. We're laughing, panting, and yelling as we both come.

I hope like hell I remembered to put the do-not-disturb sign on the door. If a maid decides to come in to do the cleaning, she'll sure get an eyeful. And the two of us might not even notice.

———

Abby

I KNOW IT HAS TO END SOMETIME. I DON'T WANT IT to. I've never been with a guy like Zach. Not that I'm Ms. Experience, or anything, but I've had a couple of boyfriends in my time. However, none like Zach.

Zach proves he knows how to make me feel good, and he puts effort into it. He doesn't expect me to lie flat so *he* can feel great and walk away. No, he takes his time, touching me, bringing my body to life.

Zach is good at bed talk too. I don't know if what he says is rehearsed, but it sounds sincere.

You know you're the most beautiful woman I ever saw, right?

I love the taste of you. I can't get enough.

I never realized before how hot a guy's tongue on my ankles would be.

We lay back in exhaustion after the third time making love. My throat is scratchy, my limbs tired, my body wonderfully loose.

"We're going to have to go downstairs soon," I say glumly. "Someone will come looking for us."

"One of my nosy brothers, probably." Zach stretches, rippling his muscles in a good way. "I should head them off."

Still we lie on the bed, reluctant to let this go. What we've had might never happen again, and we know it.

"There's this restaurant." Zach speaks offhandedly, like he has a passing thought and decides to voice it. "Mason's. On Sixteenth Street just south of Thomas. Kind of a hidden gem."

"Yeah?" I wait in anticipation.

He pauses, studying my face. I wonder what he's looking for and do my best to be interested, but not desperate. A good balance between *I'd like to see you again,* and *This was fun. If we never have anything again, this was good.*

I'm not sure I manage it.

"You should try it sometime," Zach finishes. "You know, if you ever pry yourself out of the East Valley."

"I do leave it. On occasion. For a very good reason."

We watch each other again. I'm not sure what he wants me to say, if anything. "Maybe ... uh." I choke on the word, wet my lips.

Zach waits, tense. "Maybe what?"

"Maybe we could meet there sometime."

Okay. I said it. Ball's in his court. Could be that's what he wanted.

Zach nods, as though I've spoken something profound. "Yeah. Maybe we could."

There's some relief between us now. We want to see each other again. On some unspecified day in the future. This one-night-stand might expand into another one.

Someday. Maybe.

———

Zach

WHEN I FINALLY MAKE MY WAY BACK TO MY OWN

room, ready for a shower, shave, and change of clothes, I run straight into Ben.

Ben and I are the middle kids. Neither of us have the importance of the oldest son or the adorability factor of the youngest. Austin soaks it up like a brat.

Ben and me stick together—usually. Today, my shy younger brother gives me the biggest knowing grin I've ever witnessed on him.

"Oh, man." Ben leans against the nearest wall in the hallway, arm over his stomach. "You look like you've been hit by a truck, but really, really enjoyed it."

I'm on him in a heartbeat, my fist around his shirt. "Don't you say a word. I don't care if you make fun of me, but I don't want her upset. Understand?"

"Got it." Ben pats my arm, fondly. "Your secret is safe with me." He makes the motion of a zipper over his mouth.

"Thank you." I release him and smooth the T-shirt I've wrinkled, then head for my room.

Behind me comes muffled laughter. "Bro," Ben says softly. "You have glitter in your hair."

For some reason, this makes me insanely happy.

Once I reach my room I shower, dress, and pack up my few things. I hurry to the lobby to check out, but I linger there in case Abby comes down. When she does, I can talk to her again, maybe take her to breakfast.

Except, she never shows. As I pretend to thoroughly read all the newspapers under the sunny skylight, a couple more of the bridesmaids appear. One is Brooke Marsh, who has a bad history with Austin.

He and Brooke went out for a while and now they loathe each other. I noticed they kept a wary distance from each other all through the rehearsal, rehearsal dinner, the wedding, and the reception.

I move toward Brooke, casually, as though simply returning my last newspaper to the table where I found it. This takes me close to her as she fumbles in her purse.

Brooke is stunning, and I understand why Austin chased her in the first place. She has black hair she streaks with red, an arresting face, dark skin, and eyes of deep brown. She makes anything she puts on look good, including the bicycle shorts and baggy T-shirt she wears this morning.

For all Brooke's beauty, my only interest in her today is that she and Abby are very good friends.

"Morning," Brooke says to me, giving me her sunny smile. "A McLaughlin brother I actually want to speak to."

I feign surprise. "Has Ben been talking trash to you? I'll kick his ass."

She laughs. "Poor Ben. He has to get over his too-nice disease. He lets himself be taken advantage of."

"Tell me about it. I rescue him all the time." I clear my throat. "So, how's it going?"

Brooke's smile grows wider, her beauty putting everyone else in the room to shame. Austin is an idiot.

"I know why you're sweet-talking me, Zach. Abby left already. She said she has a work project she has to finish before she goes in tomorrow. Aw." Brooke softens in sympathy as my face falls. "You don't look near as happy to see me now."

"Oh. Sorry. I just ..."

"I know what you just. You and Abby ..." Brooke scans me, dark brows arched. "Yeah, I can see it. I don't mind helping you—you're not Austin." She digs her phone from her purse. "At least there are *three* good McLaughlin brothers."

"Austin's not *so* bad." I defend him—he's my brother, right?

"Yes, he is." Brooke skims her thumb down her phone and starts typing. "I'm texting you Abby's number. Leave her be today, because she really is behind on her project, but in a few days, ask her out. Like a normal person."

"You mean instead of prying intel from her friends?"

Brooke hits *Send*, and my phone buzzes. I glance at the number and then save it to my contacts, but I don't really need to. I've already absorbed it, memorized it. The most important number on the planet.

"Exactly." Brooke's smile fades, and she gives me a stern look. "And you could have just asked me. Abby isn't going out with anyone at the moment. I mean, she was, but he's a dweeb, so good riddance."

"Thank you." I must appear pathetically grateful because Brooke smiles again and pats my arm.

"Happy to help."

"But seriously, how are you doing?" I ask. "Everything good with you? I'm not just a jerk trying to get Abby's number—I want to know."

"I'm fine. Really. I have a great life, a good job, lots of friends. Not seeing anyone and don't want to. My girlfriends and I are going on a trip together this summer—ladies only. Looking forward to it."

Her eyes hold defiance, as though she wants me to tell Austin when I see him that her life is perfect without him.

"His loss," I say. "Take care, Brooke. You're awesome."

"You're such a sweetheart." Brooke enfolds me in a warm hug. I get a kiss on the cheek as well. "Good luck," she says as she pulls away. "Abby deserves some fun. She works way too hard."

"She's not going on the trip with you?"

"We asked her, but she can't get the time off—Abby works for a total jerk. We set something up with her for later." Brooke's expression turns warning. "You be nice to her. Or a whole bunch of people will be on your ass. All right?"

"I know. One of them is now my sister-in-law."

"Yep. So be careful."

I clutch my phone like it's made of gold. "I will. See you, Brooke."

"See you around, Zach. Give Ben a kiss for me."

"Bleh. No. I'll just tell him you said hi."

She laughs, and to the merry sound, I quit the hotel. I load my bag into my pickup and let it roar to life. I sit for a time, looking at Abby's number on my phone, before I lay the phone gently aside and drive away.

———

Abby

IT's MONDAY, AND I'M SUFFOCATING IN CUBICAL hell. I spent all day Sunday and well into Sunday night trying to finish my presentation with a hangover and seriously distracted by thoughts of Zach McLaughlin. All that is making for a terrible morning today.

I want to bask. I want to sit and remember Zach touching me and kissing me, and the wonderful feel of him inside me. I recall the sense of completion I've never experienced in my life. I want to draw that to me, wrap my arms around it, not let it go.

Plus I just want to think about Zach. His eyes, his smile, his body I want to lick all over. Again. I need a full-length poster of him in my cubicle so I can gaze at him whenever I wish.

Nothing like that would be allowed. Not in this sterile office. We get one or two photos of family and that's it. Everything personal is discouraged.

My boss, Mr. Beale, is a tall, thin guy with eyes like steel ball bearings. Not one to inspire confidence. He doesn't much like women, but he has to deal with us, because there are a lot of us in the marketing and sales departments. He watched me in severe disapproval this morning while I made my presentation.

It didn't go well. Didn't I understand the product? Mr. Beale snapped at me in front of the whole department. Did I have *any* imagination at all, and could I come up with *one* single decent campaign?

Not today, sir. I have a heartache.

Will I ever see Zach again? I live way south in Chandler, almost to Sun Lakes, and his family's main office is somewhere around Seventh Street and Bethany Home, about thirty miles away through dense traffic. My chances of running into him casually are nil.

I could call him. His business, McLaughlin Renovations, is prominently listed in the phone books that still arrive in my driveway, and it's on their website. Which I don't have up on my computer *at all*. That wouldn't be allowed.

It's a decent website technically. Easy to navigate, fast—I hear that Ben McLaughlin is in charge of it. But it lacks pizazz. The marketer in me wants to redesign it with better colors, catchier photos, maybe a nice pic of the brothers and their dad and mom. People like a locally owned business with a family you can trust. Faceless corporations have become repellent.

I hear Mr. Beale's footsteps, and I quickly minimize the site on my computer. There's a ripple of consternation that spreads out as he walks down the maze, like he's a gator in a Florida swamp.

And about as cold. "Warren," he snarls at me as he halts outside my cubicle. "I need those sales materials redone before you're out of here tonight. I'm not allowed to keep you from your lunch hour but consider taking your work to the lunchroom with you."

"Okay." Nothing much else I can say.

Mr. Beale curls his lip and stomps away. I feel the relief from other cubicles as he goes. The gator isn't after them today.

Usually my job isn't bad. I like my team and co-workers, the pay is decent, and so are the benefits. I tell myself Gator-man will have to retire one day, and then we'll have a party. For us.

As I gather up my tablet computer and handouts on the new product, my phone buzzes.

I check it quickly, telling myself it might be something important from my mom. A call or text from Zach? No, that won't happen.

So why do I drop everything to snatch up the phone?

It's an email, and not from Zach or my mom. I open it in curiosity, and my eyes widen as I read it. I sit down slowly, still reading, and then I go over it twice more to make sure I'm not misunderstanding.

I hit reply and type with shaking fingers. I hesitate a few seconds with my thumb over the *Send* icon. Then I take a deep breath and tap it.

If this works out, it will change everything.

Chapter Six

Zach

"SO YOU AND ABBY HOOKED UP?" Austin asks me in the office Monday morning.

I choke on my coffee. I cough and cough, setting my cup down on the empty receptionist's desk. Friday had been Sandra, our receptionist's, last day.

Austin stands in front of me with his coffee, waiting in curiosity. He isn't condemning me. He just wants to know.

Ben, who had come out of his IT dungeon in time to hear the question, makes the zipping motion over his mouth. *I didn't tell him,* he was saying.

I didn't think he had. Ben is honest.

"What are you talking about?" I manage in reply.

Austin rolls his eyes. "Come on. The two of you doing the dirty dancing, then ignoring everyone to talk together, then disappearing after the reception. Conclusion—Zach and Abby hooked up. Am I right?"

"Yes," I say tightly. "Don't want to talk about it. None of your business."

Austin chortles. "It was good, I can tell. If it had been horrible, you wouldn't be able to shut up about it. Wallowing in disappointment."

"Disappointment about what?" says a woman's voice.

The new speaker has us three brothers straightening our backs. Virginia McLaughlin, a.k.a. Mom, comes out of her office, a sparkle in her eyes. Her firstborn has been married off, and she's ecstatic.

"Nothing," I answer quickly.

"Zach and Abby Warren," Austin supplies.

Mom turns to me. She's going on sixty, and you'd never know it. She runs three times a week, gets up early to open the office, and works harder than anyone else here. Has since she and Dad started this business when they were newlyweds. Mom does all the accounting. Once she figured out that Dad was great with clients but seriously sucked with money, she dug in and never let go. We're all very, very glad she did.

Austin shares a lot of Mom's looks, her angular face and light blue eyes, hair so dark it's almost black. Ben, me, and Ryan are more like Dad. Hard-faced, brown hair that ranges from dark to light, eyes that hide our smarts. Well, hide Ben's and Dad's smarts. Ryan and I are average. It's hell living with geniuses.

"Zach and Abby Warren what?" Mom demands.

I pick up my mug and try to hide behind it. "You saw us. We danced."

"I did see." Mom sounds interested. "And ...?"

I'm getting hot under the collar. Literally. I run my finger around my neckband. "And nothing." I am *not* discussing my sex life with my mother.

"Are you going to ask her out?"

Austin huffs into his coffee. Ben looks innocent, but he lingers, as though there's nothing in his closet of an office worth going back to.

Mom pins Austin with a severe gaze. "Something funny?"

"No, ma'am." Austin's still chuckling as he drinks his coffee.

"Well?" she asks me.

"Possibly. I have her number." I glance at Austin and decide not to tell him who gave it to me.

"Good," Mom says with conviction. "Abby's nice. I remember her from when you were kids. She was your first kiss, right?"

Austin makes more noises of hilarity, and I want to crawl behind the high reception desk and not come out. "I didn't know you knew that."

Mom sends me the pitying glance mothers get when their kids think they're so much smarter than their parents. "Ryan told me. A long time ago. I liked her. You should call her."

"I might."

Mom smiles at me, eyes warm. "It's your business, honey. I promise, I won't interfere. Much." She sweeps her glance over us all. "I assume none of you have any work to do? Funny, I thought there'd be more while Ryan's out and Sandra's gone."

"Lots." I heft my mug. "Just getting some coffee."

"I already miss Sandra," Ben says mournfully.

"We all do." I sketch a salute at the empty desk. "Champion handler of clients and the phone. But she needed to leave."

"Yeah," Austin says. "Deciding to help her single daughter raise her children. Where are people's priorities?"

Ben turns on him, outraged, but I raise a placating hand. "He's joking." I leaf through the mail stacked on the counter, pulling out correspondence and catalogs addressed to me. "At least I hope so."

"Of course I am." Now Austin is annoyed. "I'm not a dick. Oh, sorry, Mom."

"If you boys didn't swear, I'd think something was wrong with you." Mom sweeps in and takes the rest of the mail. "Now get the hell back to work."

She leaves us staring at each other awkwardly. Then we disperse.

Our main office is a showroom with the middle of the floor filled with a few demo models of custom kitchens and bathrooms, lots of sample books, and tables and chairs where we can talk with clients or people we hire to do the installation.

Offices ring the floor—Mom's is filled with computer printouts and books, Dad's with photos of remodels we've done, going back thirty years. Austin's is surprisingly pristine. Ben's is a dark, mysterious cave filled with humming machinery.

Mine has piles of books about the latest in appliances and home-improvement gadgets, plus pictures of my brothers and me at the lakes or tubing down the Salt River or in Las Vegas. I glance at one of Ryan and me, arms around each other in front of the Golden Nugget with the Fremont Street Experience going off over our heads.

"Glad you're happy," I murmur to Ryan's picture as I take my seat.

I shuffle through my mail and check my appointments for the day, but it isn't long before I have my phone out, staring at it. Abby's number is now at the top of my contacts. I've made it a favorite.

Will I ever use it? I push the phone resolutely aside and get ready for my first meeting. I'm driving out to a site, which will distract me from making calls. Of course, I can always use the phone hands-free while I drive. Damned technology.

I sigh, take up the tempting phone, and leave the office for my meeting.

————

SOMEHOW I MAKE IT THROUGH THE DAY WITHOUT calling Abby. I think about it fifty times an hour, but I resist. Helps that I'm taking up Ryan's clients in addition to my own—Austin and I have split them between ourselves.

I do a lot of driving today, but I don't mind. I'd rather be out on the road, in spite of crappy traffic and too many construction zones, than sitting behind a desk. It's why I like what I do. I see new houses and historic ones all the time, and I help people make a nice place for themselves.

Today I drop by the house we're building for people who qualify for our grant and donation program —we help those who need housing but can't afford to live in something decent. I was put in charge of the charity program, because it was my idea in the first place.

The couple who are getting our latest donation have one little boy and another kid on the way. They've come out to see what we're doing.

McLaughlin Charities searches for and buys lots in older neighborhoods where a house has maybe been torn down or abandoned. The house or lot is usually difficult for the owners to sell, or else it's been fore-closed on.

We either renovate the hell out of the existing struc-ture or simply build a new one, which is often cheaper and easier. We cover the cost and consider applicants who are the most needy but also not likely to move in with their gang and start robbing the neighbors. Folks my mom refers to as having "fallen on hard times."

I like when people are smiling and excited about moving into a new house. I talk with the dad, who is my age. His wife doesn't say much but grins at me as she holds on to her son with one hand. He wants to see everything, so I give the little guy a tour.

Ryan and Calandra will be like this in a few years, I realize, with one or two kids in tow. I'll be an uncle. A proud one.

I have a sudden flash of myself as a dad, my wife next to me, touching my arm with comfortable familiarity, like this man's wife does with him. The wife in my vision is Abby, and she holds the hand of a little girl who has brown eyes ringed with gray, like Abby's.

Holy shit, where did that come from? Abby and I had a one-night stand, for crap's sake. Not a relationship. Not even close.

I shakily say goodbye to the couple and move on to my next client, and the next. But I can't shake the vision.

I take my phone and throw it into the far corner of the back seat.

———

"WORKING LATE?" AUSTIN SAYS TO ME AS HE LEANS on my office doorway.

It's after six, and I'm typing notes into my computer, getting ready for the next day. The showroom is closed, and everyone else is gone.

"Looks that way," I grunt.

I'm avoiding going home. The phone will sit on my kitchen counter, mocking me while I slurp down take-out Kung Pau Chicken. *You want to call her, you want to call her.*

But does she want *my* call? Let's go over the facts:

When I dressed myself in her hotel room yesterday morning, Abby didn't ask me to stay. She said something about going home to work on a project for her job. I said "Okay, see you" or something equally inane before I departed.

Abby didn't tell me to wait or suggest we have breakfast together, not even room service. By the time I'd showered, packed, and reached the lobby, she'd already checked out. Brooke had told me she'd gone. Why had Brooke told me? Because she felt sorry for me, not because Abby instructed her to. If I hadn't run into Brooke, I'd never have known.

Brooke thought I should call Abby. Abby herself never said a word about calling, hadn't given me her phone number, hadn't asked for mine.

Is Abby cringing about the night she spent with me? We'd been drunk, bonding over old times, catching up, and ... that was it.

I'm not cringing at all. I want to relive every second of Saturday night, and have often, throughout the day. I got honked at or given the finger whenever I lingered at a traffic light, not noticing that red had turned to green.

Austin knocks on the doorframe, brows raised. I've drifted again. To Abby's scented skin, her leg wrapped around me, the beautiful sounds she makes as she comes ...

"Want to grab a brew?" Austin asks.

"Yes." I stand up hastily, slamming my laptop closed and shoving it aside. Ben will get on me about not logging out properly, but I don't have the patience to do it tonight. "Great idea."

Anything to keep me from being home alone with my thoughts. Watching basketball will help, but there are time-outs and commercials. Too many lulls.

"Where do you want to go?" Austin asks as I join him.

"Mason's." The name comes without thought. I'd been talking about it to Abby, so it's the first place on my mind. But why not? Mason's has the best steaks and burgers in town and also a bar with a big television. I can watch the Suns game there.

Austin blinks at my choice—we usually go to a bar down the street from here—but he shrugs. "Okay. You drive."

He does that so he can bury himself in beer and I can't, but being drunk will probably just make my thoughts more morose.

Traffic has thinned somewhat by the time we're on the road. Not entirely, but rush hour's mad crush has passed.

Our office is on a side street between Bethany Home and Missouri, about a block west of Seventh Street. It's a little off the beaten path, but we don't depend on walk-in business, so it's fine with us. A quiet street means it's easier to pull into and out of our small parking lot.

I drive south on Seventh Street for a bit and take a

left on Thomas until Sixteenth Street. South again to pull into a strip mall that's been upgraded from mid-town sag. New restaurants have come in, and a couple of shops. I park and we walk into Mason's.

The hostess recognizes us as semi-regulars, and greets us warmly. Austin pauses to flirt. I push past him to the bar and take a seat, ordering a draft beer for me and a bottled one Austin likes for him, no glass.

He joins me in a moment, hopping up onto the seat beside me, thanking me for the beer that lands in front of him. The game has already started—it's in the Midwest tonight, the Suns at the Timberwolves.

Austin glances around while I stare at the screen, semi-watching. After a few minutes, he pokes at me with the hand holding his beer.

"Hey," he says. "Isn't that Abby?"

Chapter Seven

Zach

I NEARLY FALL off my stool turning around to scan
the restaurant. It *is* Abby, sitting in a corner table in the
shadows ... with another guy.

I'm half on, half off my barstool, beer glass slack in
my hand. I'm staring like a fool, giving myself away to
Austin, the bartender, and everyone in Mason's.

For the moment, I see nothing but Abby. She's radiant. Her dark hair is pulled into a style that frames her
face, her brown eyes sparkle as she leans into the guy
and smiles at him. Abby's wearing a dress of black or
gray or dark blue—hard to tell in this light—topped
with a thin jacket, as though she's come directly from
work. The skirt bares her legs and draws my gaze
straight to them.

"Who's that with her?" Austin's next to me, his
voice in my ear.

I shrug as though I don't care, but I'm burning with curiosity and uneasiness. Is this her old boyfriend? The idiot she told me about and Brooke said she was done with? Or is it a new one?

"Want to leave?" Austin asks it casually, but I hear in his tone that he's got my back. Whether I stay or go, he'll be right beside me.

I shrug again. "Why?"

"Because the woman you slept with Saturday night is with another guy." Austin likes stating the obvious. "Because it's weird."

"It's not weird. We're not together." If I say it adamantly enough, I'll believe it.

"Okay." Austin sets his beer on the counter. "We stay. Probably you should watch the game."

Sounds like exciting things are happening on the screen. Fans are screaming, or booing. The Suns center is setting up a free throw. He's a great shooter, and he'll put them ahead again.

I can't be bothered to watch. He'll do it with me or without me. I hear the guys at the bar shouting, *Yes!* and know the throw is good.

At the same time I realize Austin is right. I can't hover on my stool and stare across the restaurant. Worried. Also drooling a little. I lift a napkin and wipe my mouth.

Abby glances up from her conversation and sees me.

I wait for her to show dismay, mortification, to turn away quickly and pretend I don't exist.

Instead, she flashes a huge smile, one that smacks me right in my heart. She waves, says something to her date, and now she's getting up, she's walking over. What the hell?

Play it cool. Play it cool. Austin's whispering the same thing, like I don't know I should.

I drop my crumpled napkin and move to meet her. We intersect halfway between the bar and the tables, far enough from the television to cut its noise, and far enough from the tables that our conversation won't be overheard.

Not that Abby keeps her voice down. While I desperately try to think of what to say, she cries, "Zach. How great to see you. I remembered you mentioning this place."

It had been in both our heads, I guess. Me for a place to mope, her for somewhere to bring her next conquest.

Abby glances past me as I stand mutely. "Austin. Hey." She waves at him. Presumably he waves back or otherwise makes a sign of greeting. I can't turn around to check.

Abby resumes gazing at me, her smile full of warmth. "How have you been?" she asks. "You know, in the last twenty-four hours or so?"

Her teasing takes me back to our warm bed, the two of us surrounded by sheets and too many pillows while we loved each other hard.

"I'm ... good. Been busy today."

"Me too."

More staring. My attempt at brilliant conversation peters out.

Again, Abby glances beyond me. Austin must be giving her signals, because she jumps.

"Oh, yeah. Come and meet Brent Savidge. He's head of marketing at Global Innovations. He wanted to talk to me somewhere not near my office, and I remembered you recommending Mason's. It's not far from the airport, so I thought ... perfect."

Brent Savidge. What kind of name is that? Sounds like a comic book supervillain genius. One who can turn into a giant flying bug. Or a porn star.

Head of marketing. Abby works in sales and marketing. The ideas finally click in my slow brain.

"Wait, is this a job interview?"

"Yes." Abby beams in animation that makes her eyes shine. "Well, sort of a preliminary interview. He's a head hunter for his company, which is international." She flashes me a card, which I assume has Brent's name on it, but her hand is at her side the next instant. "He emailed me today and asked to meet me. Isn't that great? I'd love to get out of the rat maze I work in."

Abby hadn't sounded happy with her job when she'd mentioned it. Excitement radiates from her now. I relax about her being with Brent romantically, but caution rises.

"He contacted you out of the blue?"

"Not really out of the blue. I met him at a convention last month—everyone in the business knows Brent Savidge—and hinted to him I was looking around for something better. Today he said he knows of an opening that might suit me. I couldn't wait to talk to him, so I made an appointment with him this evening. He's flying out tonight, so this is a good opportunity."

She knows what she's doing, my Abby. She nearly bounces on her toes with happiness, and it's intoxicating.

"Awesome," I say with enthusiasm. "Go back and talk to him. Don't let me screw it up for you."

Abby laughs. "You won't. Come on. I'll introduce you."

She grabs my hand. Whatever I feel about meeting Brent no longer matters. Abby's hand is in mine, and that's all that's important.

The man stands as we reach the table. He's tall, in a charcoal gray business suit—which screams he's not from around here—has wavy brown hair, and a smile full of too many straight teeth. He gleams with all those teeth. *His* face should be on the side of a bus.

"Brent Savidge," he says, shaking my hand heartily.

"Zach McLaughlin."

"Zach's one of my oldest friends," Abby tells Brent, as though it's true. "His family owns a renovation business, one of the top-rated in the Valley. They win awards and everything. Zach is also head of McLaughlin Charities."

I'm dumbfounded Abby knows all this, but Brent takes on a look of professional interest. "Great to meet you. It's hard to be a small business in a big city."

"People like dealing with locals," I say, giving the standard defense. "The personal touch."

"That's true. We're a big corporation but we like the personal touch too." Another brilliant smile. "Abby said you recommended this restaurant. She's right. It's excellent."

"Also locally owned," I point out.

He laughs, everyone's friend. "Touché."

"This is Austin, Zach's brother," Abby goes on, and I'm aware of a curious Austin by my side. "Also with the family business. He does PR and client leads."

"A man after my own heart." Brent seizes Austin's hand and they size each other up. "Can I give you my card?"

"You can, but I'm pretty happy where I am," Austin says. "I have my own office, can come and go as I please, swim in Mom and Dad's pool ..."

Brent laughs his professional laugh. "I'll give you my card anyway. You never know. I can always help you all find employees."

"True, we do need a receptionist." Austin palms the card and slides it into his pocket. He may or may not ever do anything with it. I don't worry. Whatever his quirks, Austin is utterly loyal to the family.

"What do you all do around here for fun?" Brent asks.

I wave at the television where the Suns have just stolen the ball and made a three-point shot. There's a lot of cheering and beer hoisting.

"Pretty much this," I say. "More fun when the games are at home and we're at the arena. In the summer, we go to the lakes. In the winter, to the mountains for skiing."

"Arizona is so outdoorsy." Brent nods his approval. "I'm always looking for an excuse to come here. I snowboard."

Of course he did.

"I hang out at Snowbowl all winter long," Austin said. "Snowboarding can be great up there."

I sense kindred spirits about to bond. I glance at Abby, not wanting to steal her job interview. "Get you another drink?" I offer to Brent.

He perks up, ready to accept, but he glances at his watch.

"Wish I could. Flying out at nine, so better get going. Abby, it was wonderful to talk to you." Brent shakes her hand, holding it a little longer than I like, but he's trying to be sincere. "I'll call you Wednesday. What time is good for you?"

"After work," Abby says. "If my boss knew I was talking to you, he'd fire me on the spot."

Brent looks disgusted. "If he was smart, he'd offer you a raise. There's a reason your company bleeds decent people. He should fight to keep you."

"Well aren't you a lovely man?" Abby says with a smile. "I look forward to talking to you Wednesday."

Brent finally releases Abby's hand. "Let me call a ride, and I'll be out of here. Nice to meet you Zach. Austin."

"I can drive you," Austin offers. "It's not far out of my way."

He's fibbing—Austin lives north of here, and the airport is south, but he's probably dying to talk more about snowboarding. We brothers are a disappointment to him in that area.

"Thanks. If you're sure it's not too much trouble."

"Not at all." Austin waves him to the door. Austin gives Abby a long look, a very long look, before he walks away with Brent.

Brent might be effusive with his good-byes, but he also knows when to cut them off. He lets Austin precede him out, then waves farewell, like a royal prince taking his leave.

Abby and I are on our own, standing next to the table. Staring at each other some more.

———

Abby

ZACH, THE MAN I'VE BEEN DAYDREAMING ABOUT nonstop since Sunday morning, is in front of me. I was thinking about him during my drive over, during my discussion with Brent, even during my visions of an office of my own and a secretary to help me.

I brought Brent to this restaurant not only because it was convenient for him and far from where I work, but the back of my mind told me there'd be an off chance Zach would be here. Why he would be, on a random Monday night, I didn't know, but it was a possibility.

We keep standing. People are staring at us, probably wanting us to sit down and stop blocking the television.

"So," Zach says. "Brent's a slick talker."

I nod nervously. "Yes. I know. But he's truly good, and he has the power to bring people and great jobs at his company together. I might even have my own window."

I clasp my hands and flutter my eyelashes. Zach dissolves into laughter and waves me to my chair. "Hey, gotta love a guy who can get you that."

We sit, gingerly. I'm on the edge of my seat as though I'll tackle Zach if he tries to run out the door.

"Do *you* have your own office window, Zach?" I continue playing the enchanted ninny.

"I do. With a view of the parking lot. Very exciting. Gets a little hot on a summer's day."

"I'll bet." I drop the pose and lift my half-drunk glass of wine. "But at least you can see sunshine. The sky. Cars going in and out. People. I'm in the middle of the building. I mean the exact middle. If I want to see outside, I have to take a longer than usual break and hike about half a mile."

"That's why you're jumping on Brent's offer."

"He hasn't offered anything," I say quickly. "Are you hungry? I guess I'm interrupting your dinner."

Brent had ordered starters, which he'd downed most of, because I was too keyed up to eat. Zach took in the plates and my unused silverware and signaled a waitress.

"Hey, Zach," the waitress says as she stops at our table. "Welcome back." She casts me a glance of unbridled curiosity, and I can't stop my blush. "Your usual?" She starts jotting a note even before Zach answers in the affirmative. "And for you?" she asks me.

Her smile is friendly. And again curious.

I order a chicken dish that looks nice. "Thanks," I say. Why not a salad? Because 1) I'm not a rabbit, and 2) it's very hard to daintily eat a salad in front of someone you want to impress. Stuffing recalcitrant lettuce into the corners of your mouth and chewing like a cow is not attractive.

"He hasn't offered," I repeat as the waitress strides to the kitchen. "Like I said, this was a preliminary interview. He's been talking to several people while he's in Phoenix."

Zach takes a casual sip of his beer. "You'd be leaving town if you accept?"

Is he worried? Or only interested, as a friend?

A friend who ran those big, warm hands along my waist, cradled the weight of my breasts ...

I clear my throat. "No, they have offices all over. There's one in the Scottsdale Airpark. Most likely, I'd go there."

"That wouldn't suck."

"No, it would be great."

"We do a lot of business in Scottsdale," Zach says.

He leaves it there. No *maybe we could meet for*

lunch one day. Or after work for a drink. He says nothing at all.

I can't think of a way to suggest a meet-up, so I ask him about his day. I don't want to talk about mine, which sucked until I came here. I listen, interested, as Zach describes the house their charity is renovating for a family. Zach is enthusiastic, and I warm. He has a good heart.

The food comes and we mutually decide, without words, to enjoy the meal. It's very, very good, which is why this restaurant, in an out-of-the-way strip mall, is full on a Monday night.

We linger over coffee. We don't mention the wedding, what happened Saturday night, or when, if ever, we'll get together again. We talk about what we like to do—he loves basketball, when it isn't football season, though he hasn't looked at the game on TV since we sat down. He and his brothers shoot hoops for fun on a Sunday at his folks' house. The family has a boat they take to Lake Pleasant in the summer, and he waterskis and jet-skis.

I don't do any of this. I work. In the summer I work, and I swim in my mom's pool. He says waterskiing is great—maybe I'd like to join them one time this summer?

Summer is a few months away—official summer, I mean. It will be in the 100s here soon. I noncommittally say it sounds like fun.

The waitress brings over the check. Looks a question, and Zach reaches for it.

"On me," he says. When I protest, he says, "To celebrate you maybe getting a window."

It's nice of him. I say so, and he waves it off. We dance around it, both of us doing anything to make sure this is not a date.

Once the bill is paid, Zach stands up with me. Then his face falls. "Crap. The only way Austin drove Brent to the airport is in my truck."

I blink in surprise. "I never saw you give him the keys."

"We all have keys to each other's cars. In case." Zach scans the restaurant. "I don't notice him coming back for me, the shit. I'll call him. Or Ben, if Austin can't be bothered."

He slides out his phone but I put my hand on his wrist.

"It's no problem." I try to stop my voice from shaking. "I don't mind running you home."

Chapter Eight

Zach

ABBY DRIVES me to my house in a smallish SUV that glides effortlessly into traffic. We don't say much as we go, except for me giving the occasional direction.

"Nice neighborhood," she remarks as we pull off the busy streets into a quiet road lined with large trees. "Old Phoenix. I like it."

"I restored the house," I say, trying to sound offhand. "I like old places."

"Me too." Abby takes in the bungalows set back from the road, some of them large and breathtaking, others tiny and cute. "I live in a generic apartment complex that resembles all the other generic apartment complexes in this town. Always have."

"Not a lot of choice, is there? Trust me, I've lived in them too."

She pulls into the driveway of my Craftsman style

bungalow and gazes at it in admiration. It's dark, so not much of it shows beyond the porch light, but the silhouette is obvious.

"Come in," I say rashly. "I'll give you a tour."

Abby presses her lips together. She's going to say no, that she has to get home, and it's a long drive. Just when I'm about to let her off the hook, she shoves the gear into Park and kills the engine.

"Okay. I'd love to see it."

I am out of the car so fast, I create a breeze. I'm around the SUV, opening the door and ushering Abby to her feet before she can climb down herself. She's amused with me.

I'm proud of my little house. I worked my ass off on it for years. It had been partly restored by the previous owner, but he'd given up and moved back east when the central Arizona summer got too much for him. I grew up here and know how to keep cool in the middle of a summer afternoon—you find somewhere seriously air conditioned, or submerge yourself in a swimming pool, or sleep. You go outside only early in the morning and at night and stay the hell out of the heat the rest of the day.

The front door of my house opens to a wide hall, with rooms placed around it. A staircase leads up to one bedroom and bathroom, both of which I built from scratch. It used to be an empty attic up there.

I give Abby the tour, which doesn't take long. "Living room, dining, kitchen, sun room. Guest room. I was going to make this a workroom for me, but Mom insisted I have space in case one of my brothers needs to crash. Which they do, Austin in particular. And here we have the back porch."

"This is gorgeous." Abby steps onto the wide porch with deep eaves. The back yard contains a sparkling pool in a bricked-out area, and shrubs against the walls that separate me from my neighbors.

"I'm not really into gardening," I say quickly, in case she starts praising my pruning skills. "I have guys who take care of the plants."

"It's so nice." Abby sounds admiring. "Homey."

I shrug. "I fix up houses for other people. I figured I'd do this one, and sell it if I didn't care about living in it myself. But I decided to stay."

"I can see why." She drags in a breath, the air fragrant with roses in pots along the walkways. Roses bloom like a riot in April around here. By June they'll be cringing down to whimper in the heat.

"I like it." My words belie the days and weeks of sanding, sawing, hammering, drilling, and cursing. When I say I fixed up the house myself, I mean with my own two hands. I didn't hire a team and stand back and watch.

Abby turns around, resting her hands behind her on the square railing. She's relaxed, giving me a half smile, her breasts pushed toward me. She looks perfect on this porch, framed in moonlight. This house is a snapshot of the past married to the beauty of the present, like Abby herself.

And when did I start writing poetry? "I have this

bottle of Glenfiddich I've been saving ..." I hear myself say.

Abby comes out of her sexy pose and raises her hands. "Remember what happened last time we drank Scotch. And then wine."

"I'm remembering it." My smile pulls at my face. "Not regretting it."

Abby studies me a second, then lowers her arms. "I'm not regretting it either," she says softly.

My heart starts beating hard, and the heat that hasn't left me since I got out of her bed ramps up. I take her hand.

"Tour's not done yet."

She wraps her fingers around mine, the glow in her eyes spinning fire through my body. I guide her inside and then to the stairs. I installed these, though I did order them custom built—polished wood, wide steps, Craftsman bannister. Not a big staircase, but it brings us to my bedroom.

I'm glad I'd made my bed this morning, though for me that's shaking the sheets and mismatched blankets straight. Abby doesn't glance at the bed, but at the three windows that give out over the porch roof to a decent view.

"Look at the lights." She wanders to a window, and I decide not to snap on the overhead. Through a break in the trees behind the neighbor's roof, we can see the lights of Phoenix stretching south until they run into the dark wall of South Mountain. Red lights blink lazily on top of that, warning planes away from the microwave and radio towers.

I move behind her, sliding my arms around her waist. She doesn't throw me off or step away, she relaxes into me. I nuzzle her neck, inhaling her beautiful scent.

Abby lets out a sigh, as though she's perfectly content in my arms.

I'm content too ... and more than a little hungry for her. The nuzzling becomes kisses, and tiny nips. Abby lets out a soft moan and turns in my arms, seeking my lips with hers.

We enjoy a long, tongue-tangling, scorching kiss. When we're done, she's crushed against me, my hands under her jacket, looking for the zipper on her dress.

"I've been thinking about you all day," she whispers. "All day yesterday too."

"You disappeared on me." I kiss her cheek. "Checked out. Gone."

Her skin flushes beneath my lips. "I thought you wouldn't want to see me. You know ... after."

"Why the hell wouldn't I?" I growl and gently bite her chin. "I'd just made love to the most beautiful woman in the universe. Of course I wanted to see you."

She gives me a sly glance. "Didn't notice you calling me."

I could say I didn't have her phone number, but that was a lie, thanks to Brooke.

"I didn't think you'd want to talk to *me*," I counter.

"You're the most beautiful woman in the universe, remember? I'm ... Zach."

"The very hot Zach McLaughlin?" She lifts her arms and twines them around me. "I saw all the women looking at you in the restaurant tonight. Wanting to tackle me and take my place."

I knew she had to be joking. "Nah, they were looking at Austin. He attracts attention."

"Bull." Abby slides against me, and my thoughts scatter. "This was after Austin left. But it doesn't matter. We're here now."

"True." I kiss her again. "Here. Now."

That's all that matters.

Our clothes start coming off. I find the zipper and the dress loosens. I help her pull off the jacket, and the top of the sleeveless dress slides down her arms, revealing a black lacy bra.

Her hands are busy unbuckling my belt, unzipping my pants. I suck in a breath as her fingers find my cock, which is plenty stiff.

"Oh, man." I let out the breath, which sounds hoarse. "I don't think I can stand up for this."

Before she can speak, I sweep her off her feet and into my arms, heading for the bed.

Sounds easy, right? In the movies, the hero lifts the heroine like its nothing and runs with her somewhere. I saw one dude run all the way up the stairs with his lady.

In reality, it's hard to catch my balance without bouncing her, and as soon as she lets go of me, my pants fall. I trip over them, but thankfully the bed is nearby, and we land safely on it. Abby's laughing at me once again.

I kick out of my pants and shoes, and roll over to her. She's on her side, tugging at the hem of my shirt. It's a polo shirt, which I wear to look professional for clients. I drag it off over my head then the T-shirt beneath it.

Her turn. I unhook her bra, which drops off. Not waiting, I cup her breasts then lower my head and close my lips over her nipple.

Abby arches into my mouth, and I feast on the velvet softness of her. Her fingers rest again on my cock, stroking it through my underwear, sending fires through my body.

I need her. I've been thinking about her since I woke up yesterday morning, and the time between hasn't dampened my wanting. I'm dying for her.

I push her into the mattress, continuing to suckle her. She skims her fingertips up and down my cock, which jerks, ready to be inside her.

I need to get rid of the underwear. I release her, grab the elastic, and wrestle the stupid boxer briefs down my legs. The band twangs, and the briefs go flying somewhere across the room. I'm glad the window's shut, or they might have taken off into the neighbor's yard. Or landed in the pool. Or the neighbor's pool.

I scramble off the bed and into the bathroom, pawing through the drawers in search of condoms. I should have one or two left over from the past. They haven't expired yet, so I grab one and dash into the bedroom.

Abby's underwear is gone by the time I make it to her again. Probably neatly folded beside the bed. I rip open the condom packet, the wrapper flying to join my underwear.

She helps me put on the condom. This fans the flames, and I can barely breathe.

I come down on Abby, sliding one hand beneath her supple body to lift her hips to me. I position myself and slide inside her.

There. *Damn.*

We fit so well, like a key in the right lock. I stop and stare down at her, deep into brown eyes that hold the answer to happiness.

I'm so glad I found you again, Abby.

A soft noise comes from my throat, and Abby smiles at me.

I groan and start to love her. Slowly at first, then faster, faster, as we both catch the rhythm and move together.

Outside, a mockingbird starts to sing, its many calls following one after the other. The guy is pouring his heart out, trying to attract lady mockingbirds to his side.

Inside, all is quiet, except for Abby and me. She's not shy about her cries of joy, telling me exactly how good she feels and how much she loves what we're doing.

I respond, less coherently. I'm burning—she's

quenching my thirst. My body floods with icy excitement, like I'm soaring over the top of a mountain, every beat of my heart better than the last. I reach the peak and yell as I start coming down the other side.

I drive into her, and Abby holds me the whole time. She's yelling too, telling me I'm amazing, and hot, and other flattering things.

I kiss her but the two of us are too frenzied to make it romantic. I fall onto her, my hips moving, my heart full.

Abby catches me and brings me safely in for a landing. And then we're both breathless, laughing, kissing, touching, stroking. Happy. Loving.

This night is perfect.

———

Abby

I LET OUT A GROAN—NOT ONE OF PASSION—AND press a hand to my rat's nest of hair. "I should go."

It's late. Very late. I'm in Zach McLaughlin's bed, and we've made love maybe four times, each of them better than the last. So good, I've lost count.

Zach's pillow cradles my head, and he lies next to me on his side, lazily brushing a hand across my abdomen.

"Why should you?" Zach caresses my breast with the backs of his fingers.

"I have to work in the morning." I say it with sorrow.

"So do I." Zach's smile undoes something inside me.

"It's a long drive home."

"I know." Zach's strokes become warmer. "Like hell I want you to drive across a big dangerous city alone at night. Stay here. Stay safe."

Until daybreak, when traffic clogs every artery in this town. It will be an arduous crawl back to the East Valley. Not looking forward to that.

On the other hand, Zach's bed is comfortable, and he's in it with me. I yawn, pressing my fingers to my mouth.

"I might be able to stay a little longer."

"Good." He says it like a purr, and kisses my shoulder. "Stay as long as you like."

My heart trips. I suddenly yearn for his wish to extend past this night, that he wants me in this wonderful house with him for the rest of our lives.

He can't really mean that. He meant until morning, until after breakfast, when we'd go our separate ways. This will be another one-night-stand. Can you have more than one with the same person in three days?

I force myself to not ask questions. I have Zach for the right now. I draw my finger along his cheek, brushing his lips. He leans down and kisses me, and we get lost again, in the night and the moment.

When I wake once more, daylight pours through the window and Zach is gone.

I lie still for a time, waiting for feeling to return to my body, thoughts to my head. Then I sit up in a hurry.

Sunshine fills the room, windows in three directions letting it in. Sunlight gleams on the white-painted paneled walls, the simple wooden furniture, the hardwood floor scattered with throw rugs.

My clothes are in a neat pile on top of the dresser. Did Zach do that? Or does he have a maid I now have to be embarrassed in front of?

I smell coffee. Heavenly coffee. And the smell of bacon frying.

I could sit here and debate, or I could get up and have some coffee and breakfast.

I slide out of bed and snatch up my underwear. The dresser contains photos, which I see once I move my dress. Zach has pictures of his family here, some of them at a desert lake on a boat. One with his dad and mom, then the four brothers together: Ryan, Zach, Ben, Austin. They're laughing and goofing, Austin with one hand raised.

The photo captures their personalities well. Ryan, chin lifted. He's the oldest brother and has to keep these guys in line. Ben, with his shy smile. Austin, daring anyone to get in his way. And Zach ...

Zach is smiling, indulgent of his brothers, warmth in his eyes. He's happy with his family, with his life, with his choices. A rare thing to see.

I'm not settled with anything. Searching—for what, I don't know. I have good friends, a mom I love with all my being, a decent job, and prospects for another. I know I'm selfish for feeling empty, but the desolation in my heart as I contemplate returning to my own life smacks me. I want to cry.

I stop the tears by pulling on my clothes, zipping into the bathroom to wash my face and to try to pat my hair into place.

I finally go downstairs, following my nose to the kitchen. It's a large room, as kitchens are in old houses, instead of a galley attached to a dining area or family room. A table stands here, real plates set out, and silverware.

There's no maid in sight, just Zach with a spatula. He shoves a cup of coffee under my nose, which I take, and I gulp coffee gratefully.

"Breakfast?" he asks. "I did bacon and eggs. I hope that's okay with you."

"It is. But I really don't have time ..."

"Everyone has time for breakfast. It's still early. We expended a lot of energy last night." Zach laughs and kisses me on the cheek, comfortable with us.

I decide to enjoy letting a hot man fix me breakfast. Zach tells me to grab whatever I want, so I root in the refrigerator for butter for the toast, salsa for the eggs. He's well stocked.

"Does your mom go shopping for you?" I ask.

"Hey, men can know about food. My mom never was much of a cook—she's obsessed with accounting and numbers. She's like Ben—can be absorbed in her job until she doesn't realize the sun is down. My dad does the cooking, and my brothers and I figured it out when we moved into our own places."

As he speaks, he serves me up scrambled eggs and crisp bacon, toast finished to perfection—not too dry, not too limp and cold.

Zach sits next to me as I shovel it all in, worrying about the time. Zach eats with more restraint. He's a great cook, of breakfast anyway, and I force myself to slow down and savor it.

"I'll cook dinner for you some night," Zach says, fingers resting on his coffee mug.

My heart flutters. "Do you do gourmet stuff like Crepes Suzette? Whatever those are."

"Nope. My cooking is pretty plain. Steak and potatoes. Burgers. I can put together a decent salad when I want to. And I make a mean soup of leftovers."

"Sounds awesome. I don't cook much, sorry."

Zach shrugs. "Why sorry? The old days when you had to cook because you were a girl are gone. At least they are in my family."

I relax. "My family too. My mom and I perfected the art of take-out. We know how to get what we want from almost any restaurant in town any time."

He chuckles. "Yeah, I love that."

We talk about our favorite restaurants, which new ones we like, and the great ones we were sad to see go. You can tell a native of Phoenix, because we refer to places by what used to be there instead of what's there now. New is not necessarily better, but it's not rejected either.

After a while, I let out a heavy sigh. "I really should go. I'm going to be late."

Zach is resigned. "I guess you should. If *I'm* late, I get reamed out by my mom. That's the problem with a family business—everything is personal."

"Sounds nice," I say with longing.

Zach watches me a moment. "I might call you. No —I *will* call you. Today. If you don't want me to, or you think it's too soon, all you have to do is let it go to voicemail. I'll figure it out."

My heart hammers, joy flooding out my worries. "I'll pick up." I grimace. "As long as I'm not in the bathroom. I'm not a toilet talker."

"Whew!" Zach dramatically wipes his forehead. "Neither am I. Last thing I want to hear when I'm pouring out my heart is a toilet flushing."

We start laughing and can't stop. I get up and so does he, and we hang on each other, gone in hysteria.

Zach walks me to my car. A few neighbors are out, picking up newspapers or getting into cars for work. They wave to Zach, and he waves back, unembarrassed about emerging with a woman who has obviously spent the night.

He even kisses me in front of everyone. "Have a great day, Abby."

I know I will, because he's said so.

I finally make myself get into the car. "Wait—how will *you* get to work?" Zach's truck is nowhere in sight.

"I called Austin when I got up. He'll swing by."

He says it with confidence, knowing his brothers have his back at every turn.

Zach leans down and kisses me through the open window. Then he pats the top of my car and waves me off.

I drive down the road, wanting to sing. I turn on the radio, find something I can sing with, and start wailing. I turn off onto Central, heading south with everyone else in Phoenix.

The crawl to my house takes forever, as I knew it would, but I cease caring. I sing, I smile at people hunched in their cars with road rage in their eyes, wave cars to go ahead of me when they're stuck, and generally enjoy the commute.

At home I jump through a shower and dress. I could have showered at Zach's and driven straight to work, but arriving in the clothes I wore yesterday would have embarrassed the hell out of me.

My shift starts at 8:30, and I make it, miracle of miracles, at 8:40.

"Warren!" Mr. Beale yells down the cubicle alley the minute I scuttle into mine. "My office. Now!"

Chapter Nine

Zach

AUSTIN SHOWS up in my truck, which he's taken good care of. As he drives us to work, he keeps flashing me an annoying grin.

"What?" I finally ask, irritable. I don't want to interrupt my constant thoughts of Abby and our time in bed together.

"I haven't seen you this gone in a while." Austin gives me a satisfied glance. "I like it."

"*Gone*? What kind of bullshit is that?"

But I know he's right. I'm out the other side of gone and off over the horizon. I still feel Abby beneath me, her body moving with mine—one time she was on top, beautiful as she rocked on me. I stifle a groan, and Austin laughs louder.

"Oh man, your face. So are you and Abby together now, or what?"

"Two dates," I growl. "And they weren't really dates. Mind your own business, little bro."

Austin lays off, but he's still laughing under his breath.

We arrive at the office and he slams out of the truck and inside, me on his heels. I don't want him announcing in the middle of the showroom that I slept with Abby last night.

Austin stops short when we walk inside, and I nearly run into him.

Mom is at the reception desk with a young woman who has light brown hair pulled back into a bun. She's slender but not skinny, athletic but not muscle-bound. She wears glasses with light blue rims that match her eyes.

Mom turns around when we come in. "Good morning. I want you to meet Erin Dixon. The temp agency sent her. She's going to be filling in at reception for a while."

Erin smiles and says hello. Austin checks her out, but she doesn't appear to notice him beyond politeness. Interesting.

And a relief. Erin is pretty, and if Mom hired her, even as a temp, it means she's good. We don't need Austin breaking her heart.

"Glad to have you on board," I say neutrally.

"Likewise," Austin says.

Mom gives Austin a look. He touches two fingers to his forehead in salute and moves to his office.

Ben emerges from his dark den, head bent over the tablet in his hand. He moves purposefully toward the front desk, eyes on whatever the hell is so important on his device.

"Ben will set up your computer," Mom says to Erin. "He'll get you logged in and explain our phone and message system. Ben, this is Erin."

Ben drags his attention from his fascinating tablet and lands it on Erin. She smiles.

He stops. He goes so completely still his fingers are arrested in mid-tap. Mouth open, eyes fixed. Erin widens her smile.

"Uh," Ben says.

"Hi." Erin gives him a shy look, wrinkling her nose in an adorable way. Ben turns the shade of a clay brick.

If Mom notices, she says nothing. "Our system is pretty simple. Ben should be able to show you everything by lunch. If you have questions after that you can ask me, or Ben. I'll leave you to it for now."

She bustles away, scooping up her mail as she goes.

I linger, picking through the rest of the mail. Ben remains motionless. I deliberately bump into him.

"Uh ..."

"Guess I'd better get to work," I say. "Nice to meet you, Erin. If I get any calls, just put them through. I never hide. You should get started, Ben, before Mom cracks the whip."

Erin sits down, fingers resting lightly on the mouse. "So, Ben, how do I log in?"

Ben gulps and finally scuttles around the reception desk to her. I walk off to find coffee, chuckling to myself, letting Ben suffer on his own.

———

Abby

I ANSWER THE PHONE AFTER ONE RING.

"You on the toilet?" Zach asks cautiously.

"No, eating lunch." I stab at the lettuce on my leafy-green salad, my penance for the eggs and bacon at breakfast and the chicken last night. "I wouldn't have answered, remember?"

"Just thought I'd check. How are you?"

"Me? Great." I don't tell him Mr. Beale yelled at me for twenty minutes for being ten minutes late. Result, I'm taking a short lunch and will be staying after work.

"I'm great too." His voice is low, sultry, holding notes of what we shared last night.

I forget all about my salad, Mr. Beale's stinging reprimands, my painful workload. I remember Zach, his hands on my body, the heat of his lips, the way his face smooths out when he comes.

I wonder what he's called about, what he wants to ask. But Zach asks nothing. He just talks. Tells me about the new temp and how Ben nearly swallowed his tongue when he saw her. How his charity house is coming. He then asks about my mom, my work, what I'm doing. Like he's interested.

We talk, we laugh. I stretch out my legs under the table in the empty lunchroom and give myself over to conversation. I haven't done that, especially not with a guy, in a long time. Well, with a guy, never.

My lunch comes to an end and I regretfully say good-bye. We don't make any plans to see each other again. Or to talk again.

But it doesn't matter. With Zach I feel like I don't have to be desperate. I don't have to have a plan, a schedule, reassurance that I'll see him. I know I will. What we have is just ...

I give up trying to explain it to myself and return to my sterile cubicle. But the call has changed my attitude. The stress of trying to figure out how to sell a plastic thing that holds another plastic thing, to a business that makes bigger plastic things, lifts. It's fun, like it used to be.

I stay my extra ten minutes after work to make Mr. Beale happy, and twenty minutes after that—I'm so absorbed in my projects.

Then I go home to my empty apartment and fill it with thoughts of Zach.

Am I heading for a crash? Heartache that will be worse than my bored loneliness?

I don't know, and for this moment, I don't care. Zach doesn't call tonight though I leave the phone next to me wherever I am. Still, I don't care. This afterglow is going to last a long, long time.

―――――

Zach

AUSTIN SAYS I'M STALKING HER, BUT I CAN'T HELP it. I call Abby at least once every day. I don't give a shit what we talk about—I just want to hear her voice.

I stop calling her during lunch because I figure she'll want to eat her lunch. I wait until she's home, in casual shorts and tank top, relaxing with a glass of wine, and then I call. I know that's where she'll be, because I've asked her to tell me what she likes to do after work, how she unwinds, what she's wearing ...

Okay, maybe I *am* stalking her.

I start texting her after I think this, warning her I'll call, so she has the chance not to answer.

She always texts back saying she's looking forward to it.

We don't make any plans. No dates or hook-ups. I don't know what we're doing, but we keep doing it. One day I'm going to drive over and show up at her door. She can slam it in my face or invite me in for talking or ... whatever happens.

I've never had a relationship that I played by ear. Always there was *Where is this going? Are we exclusive? No, Zach, I can't go out for drinks right now, because I'm in bed with another guy.*

That last one could only happen to me.

For some reason I don't worry Abby will be with another guy when I call. I *should* be worried—she's attractive, funny, and has her own life. Guys ought to be beating down her door.

Austin thinks my sort-of relationship with Abby is highly amusing. At the family dinner on Sunday, Mom asks why Abby hasn't come with me. I scan the table, taking in my two brothers and my parents and their interested faces, and shake my head. Because they'd grill her, that's why. And assume she's staying in my life forever.

"Didn't you used to go with her before?" Ben asks. "In high school?"

"Junior high," Austin answers with glee. "He was in *love*. He'd sing dopey songs into his hairbrush."

"I was *thirteen*," I say with heat. "Doesn't explain why *you* still do it."

Ben busts up laughing. Austin gives him the eye, and I know he's going to start teasing Ben about Erin. Ben can barely talk to the woman, though he's been at her desk every day, explaining the software and fixing little things that go wrong. We've never had so many glitches.

"I talked to Brooke day after the wedding," I slide in, pretending I'm going for neutral conversation. "She's doing good."

Austin gives me a *that's-below-the-belt* scowl.

"I like Brooke," Mom says, taking another helping of roasted potatoes. "I remember her when she was younger—I always said she'd do well. She manages an auto business, did you know that?"

Abby has mentioned it. Brooke sells luxury cars—

she'd originally been hired to attract men to buy cars they didn't need, but she'd turned that around and been so good at the business she'd become manager in no time at all. Now she's talking about buying the business when its owner retires.

Austin retreats, suddenly absorbed in his food. Ben shoots me a look of gratitude.

Talk turns to Ryan and Calandra. They'll be home next week.

"We'll have a big dinner to celebrate," Mom says. "Zach, why don't you invite Abby?"

I choke on the bite of steak I've shoved into my mouth. I cough, drink water. "I'm not sure she'll be interested," I manage.

"Why not? Calandra's her best friend. We can welcome her into the family." Mom doesn't specify whether she means Calandra or Abby, and I don't ask.

Austin doesn't either, because he's sitting there terrified Mom will suggest we invite Brooke too.

"And Erin, if she has time," Mom goes on relentlessly. "She's a nice girl, don't you think? I would like to hire her permanently, but I'm not sure she'd accept. Did you all know she's a dancer?"

Ben hasn't mentioned this. He says nothing and takes a careful sip of iced tea.

"A dancer?" I prompt.

"With the West Valley Ballet. They're not big but very, very good, from what I hear. Hard to get into. When I interviewed her, Erin explained she couldn't work anything but very set hours, because she has to rehearse and do performances. I said that would be all right."

Mom sends the rest of us a stern gaze, which means no one had better object. Ben returns to his food, not looking at anyone. Poor guy.

Dad, who long ago decided to sit back and let Mom talk, watches her in his quiet way, a smile on his face. He never says a lot, but when he does speak, we all sit up and listen.

"It'll be good to have Ryan home," he says.

He doesn't mean that to be detrimental to the rest of his sons. We agree. It will be great to see Ryan again.

"Then it's settled," Mom says. "I'll invite Erin, if she's free, and Zach will call Abby."

She reaches over and squeezes Dad's hand, everything all right in her world. Dad gives her a fond look. Everything's right in his world too.

———

Abby

IT'S THE WORST FRIDAY OF MY LIFE. I'VE BEEN given three extra projects this week, because someone on my team quit. Mr. Beale seems to think it's my fault she quit—and it is, actually. She was so miserable, I encouraged her to find another job, and she did.

The result—I have to take over all her projects. To

be done by next Monday. No way. I know I'll be coming in Saturday to finish.

Sunday, I'm supposed to drive to Zach's parents' house for a welcome-home party for Calandra and Ryan. Zach asked me hesitantly, as if the last thing I'd want to do on a Sunday afternoon was spend time with him and his family.

I accepted without question.

Now I fear I'll have to cancel. If I don't get these presentations done before Monday morning, we'll lose the accounts, and it will be on me.

At five-thirty, when I'm supposed to be heading out, Mr. Beale decides to jump on my ass.

"I want that done before you leave today, Warren."

The projects will take me many hours—I know this from experience.

"I plan to come in over the weekend, Mr. Beale, plus work on the projects at home too. Everything will be done by Monday."

"No—I want them on my desk *tonight*." He glowers at me, towering over my cubicle wall.

Mr. Beale never, ever approaches me closer than six feet, never touches me, never does anything to break any rule about harassment. Never curses, or says a wrong word that could be construed as belittling me because of my gender. He treats us all like faceless robots.

But he finds his own ways, totally within the rules, to be intimidating.

"I can only work so fast." I try to keep the rage out of my voice.

"You find plenty of time to talk to your friends. Tonight, before you walk out. Or don't come in on Monday."

"Mr. Beale ..."

"Fine." He takes two steps back. "But I expect to see you in here all day tomorrow and all day Sunday."

"Like I said." I can't be bothered to be polite. Since I'm a salaried employee, this means no overtime. I draw the same pay whether I work forty hours or eighty.

"Good." He turns and stalks off.

I refuse to burst into tears, but I want to.

I reach for the phone to call Zach and explain why I can't be at the party. If I do it quickly, it will hurt less.

The phone rings before I touch it. The readout shows it isn't Zach.

I snatch up the phone. "Hello?"

"Hey there," Brent Savidge says. "Bad time?"

"Wonderful time. How are you?"

"I'm great, but you're about to be better. How'd you like a forty-thousand dollar a year raise? And your own office with a great view?"

"I would love it." I want to cry again, but in relief. I haven't heard from Brent since our dinner, and I'd assumed I hadn't landed the job. "You don't know how much."

"Awesome. I'll be in Phoenix Monday, and we can talk. That okay with you?"

"Perfect." I wouldn't be at this job Monday, so I'd

have all day. *Mr. Beale—I quit!* That was going to feel good to say.

"Looking forward to it. Oh, and Abby ..."

I listen to what Brent tells me, not sure I'm hearing right. Three weeks ago, his words wouldn't have mattered, and I'd be dancing on the moon. Today ...

Today, I don't know what to do.

Chapter Ten

Zach

RYAN AND CALANDRA return to town Friday afternoon, arriving at the office for their grand entrance before heading to their own place.

No clients are there, so we congregate in the open showroom. Mom hugs Ryan then Calandra, then Ryan again, tears on her face.

"Good to see you, bro." I give Ryan a hard hug, crushing him. I've missed my big brother, always there with advice. I should talk to him, but I don't want to monopolize his time while he's busy being adored.

Ben hugs Ryan with much back-pounding, then Austin comes in for his. We all get to hug Calandra too —she's our sis now. Erin hangs back, as she's not part of the family, trying to give us our space. Mom, however, introduces her, and both Calandra and Ryan greet her with enthusiasm.

It's a while before Ryan can wander into the break room by himself. Austin and I are in there grabbing coffee, and I pour Ryan a cup.

"Glad to be back?" I ask him.

Ryan snorts as he lifts his coffee. "Back to work instead of days of blissful ease in the wilderness with my lady? Sure."

I toast him with my cup. "I hear you. So what did you guys do?"

"They had sex." Austin leans on the counter, coffee in hand, grinning. "What do you think?"

Ryan flushes, but he doesn't deny it or look ashamed.

"I meant in between the sex," I clarify.

"It was beautiful. We hiked through slot canyons and fields yellow with wildflowers, found an old railroad bridge and ancient pueblo ruins. It was cool."

Ryan loved that kind of thing—hiking over Arizona and discovering out-of-the-way bits of it. History and wild land. Now he had someone special to share those adventures with.

"What's been going on here?" Ryan asks. "Besides the usual."

"Zach's sleeping with Abby Warren," Austin answers promptly.

I take a swing at Austin, but he's adept at avoiding me.

Ryan's brows climb. "Yeah? She's Calandra's best friend. Don't let me hear that blowback when you break her heart."

I frown at him. "Why are you so sure she'll be the one with the broken heart?"

"I know you, Zach. You aren't easily satisfied. A woman wants a commitment, and you don't commit."

"It's mutual drifting," I say in my defense. "Or the lady decides she prefers someone else." Ryan nods in sympathy, knowing what I'd gone through. "Besides, who are you to talk about running from commitment?"

"Okay, so I learned my lesson." Ryan's contented smile tells us he's plenty reconciled to being married to Calandra. All the sex under the stars probably hadn't hurt. "But if you're not sure about Abby, break it cleanly and stay friends, so my wife doesn't jump all over my case about it."

The proud shine in his eyes when he says the words *my wife* have me and Austin busting up laughing. We have to hold on to each other, we're laughing so hard.

Ryan tells us we're assholes and walks out. But making fun of our oldest brother is why we get up in the morning.

I'm glad he's back, so we can keep doing it.

———

Abby

WHEN I PULL INTO THE DRIVEWAY OF THE McLaughlin house off Central and Glendale, I gape, overwhelmed.

It's an older property with a wide spread of land and towering old-growth trees. I live in a part of the city that was developed in the late 90s, the houses and apartments exactly the same, the landscaping sparse. *This* is Phoenix of a hundred years ago, when people sought shade and built houses with deep porches, in quest of coolness whenever they could find it. It's an abode from the time before air conditioning and insulation changed the face of the city.

The house sprawls across the grounds in Spanish Mission revival style, which means lots of arches, stucco, and tile. It rises two stories, the second floor peeping out here and there instead of in one block. Bougainvillea, blooming in a riot of fuchsia, salmon, and scarlet, crawls up the walls in the sunny areas, and dark green citrus trees stand in a regimented line in one corner.

The drive is paved with brick and holds many cars and SUVs. A big welcome-home party. I see Zach's pickup, and my heart sinks.

It took me a long time to decide to come. I debated about staying the hell home and preparing myself for a new life, but in the end, I knew I had to face Zach. I owe him that. Plus, Calandra would never let me hear the end of it when she found out.

I pick up the basket of wine and goodies I've brought for the returning couple, straighten my sleeveless dress, and leave the car. Zach mentioned that the pool would be ready for swimming, but I feel vulnerable enough without people staring at me in a bathing suit.

Noise leads me through a side gate to the backyard, which is humongous. More bricks pave the way to the pool, which shimmers in cool blue invitation across the yard. Another area of grass stretches alongside the house, and I can imagine the four McLaughlin brothers as kids running wild on it. Calandra and Ryan's children will play there someday.

My heart is heavy, but I put on a smile and walk toward Calandra, who lets out a squeal when she sees me. Ryan, next to her, rescues the basket that falls from my arm while Calandra and I hug it out.

Calandra looks amazing. Her blue eyes glow, and she's relaxed, happy. The way she leans into Ryan means the rest of us had been right. They were meant for each other.

I quickly embrace Ryan and start joking with the two of them so I won't weep. I'm so happy to see Calandra and very sad for myself, but I hold it together.

Calandra links arms with me and we wander toward the open green, while Ryan totes the basket into the house. The yard is filled with people, mostly McLaughlins, including Zach's Great Aunt Mary. The slender young woman Ben keeps staring at must be Erin Dixon, the temp Zach has told me about.

"So ... you and Zach." Calandra turns me around as soon as we're out of earshot of the rest of the party. "Tell me everything."

"Nothing to tell." I shrug. "We've been out a few times."

"Look me in the eye when you say that."

I raise my head and meet her wise gaze. I slump. "I've fallen in love with him." The words wrench out of me, and I know each one is true. "What am I going to do? It's stupid. Our only connection is we knew each other as kids. Briefly. He has his own life. I have to get on with mine."

Calandra's smile vanishes as she feels my misery. "Oh, honey." She gathers me into a hug, this woman who's been my friend for ages. "There's more going on, isn't there? Tell me."

I find comfort crying on her shoulder and don't want to raise my head. Calandra takes hold of my arms and forces us apart. "People will stare. Stand up straight and tell me everything."

She's right, and I do. When I'm finished, wiping my eyes on a tissue she hands me, Calandra says sternly, "Go talk to Zach."

I shake my head. "I know it will be over when I do. I thought maybe I could have this day to enjoy myself, and then tell him."

"Nope. For one, you're not enjoying yourself. You're sobbing into a soggy tissue. Second, it's not fair to Zach. I bet you were just going to wave at him today without saying a word, and then vanish. Easier for you, sure. But not for the rest of us."

"Easier?" I wipe my eyes and let anger push away

my sadness. "It won't be easy to say good-bye to Zach, or to walk away from him. Believe me."

"Why don't you ask his opinion? Let me tell you something, honey, if you give Zach the cold shoulder, he'll tell Ryan all about it, and then Ryan will be up in my face for letting my best friend dump his brother. I don't want to start my marriage fighting about you two."

"You don't need to." I draw myself up, smoothing my hair into place. "This is between Zach and me. No one else."

"Then make it between you two." Calandra softens. "Sweetie, if you hadn't been a hard-ass with me, I wouldn't be married to Ryan and so much in love. I mean crazy in love. I'm so happy I could scream. And I have, according to Ryan." She grins, eyes alight. Any moroseness or fear she showed before the wedding has vanished. "So I'm going to be a hard-ass on you. Go. Talk to Zach. Now."

She points at the house, finger rigid. I sigh. I don't want to face Zach, but I know she's right. If I'm not up front with him, I'll regret it the rest of my life.

I seize Calandra in another hug, pointing finger and all, and kiss her cheek. "Wish me luck," I whisper.

"You won't need it," she assures me, and I wish I can believe her.

I turn on my heel and march toward the charming, welcoming house.

———

Zach

I watch Abby arrive and almost immediately be enveloped by Calandra—I figure the two will want some time to hug, talk for a year, whatever.

Out of the corner of my eye I see her walk away with Calandra toward the grassy part of the yard where I spent my young years playing football with my brothers—it's where I learned the art of the tackle and intercepting the long pass.

Calandra and Abby disappear for a bit, then reemerge. Abby starts toward the house, determination in every stride.

I make a vague excuse to Austin and my buddies and head to intercept her before anyone else can.

"Hey there," I say when I reach her. "Glad you could make it."

I never spoke a truer word. Seeing Abby after not seeing her for two weeks is like a warm spring after a long, cold winter. Talking to her on the phone every day has been fantastic, but nothing like being next to her.

Abby lifts her head, and I see profound sorrow in her eyes. I touch her arm. "What's the matter?"

"Zach ... can we talk?"

Uh-oh. The three little words no guy wants to hear. My chest suddenly feels like someone dumped a load of bricks on it.

"Sure," I say, sounding stupidly cheerful. "Come on."

I take her hand and sneak her upstairs. Well, not exactly *sneak*. Austin sees us go. He opens his mouth to draw attention, but he catches my eye and closes it again. Sometimes my little brother can be astute, and compassionate.

I lead Abby down the hall to my old room. Dad has long since made it into a library for himself, but whenever I need a retreat in the house, I gravitate here.

I close the door against the noise downstairs, additionally muffled by Dad's books and desk full of papers. Abby starts to speak, but I forestall her by drawing her into my arms.

Am I trying to stop her breaking up with me? Or comforting her? Or do I just want to touch her, breathe her in, have her against me?

All three, I think.

"I quit my job." Abby's voice is muffled in my shirt.

I rub her back. "Oh." We're silent a moment. "Help me out here. Isn't this a good thing? Or is it bad? Do I congratulate you? Or commiserate? If you want honesty, I think you're better than that soul-sucking job that was making you unhappy." I've already had some thoughts on that.

Abby raises her head, wiping her eyes. "Walking into Mr. Beale's office and saying, more or less, *You can't fire me—I quit* was awesome." A tiny smile flits across her face.

"Then it's a good thing." I swallow. "Is this what you wanted to tell me? If so, I can jump up and punch the air now."

She shakes her head, which brings back the specter of worry. "Brent also called me. You remember Brent? The head-hunter? Well, he offered me a job at his company."

She doesn't look as happy as she should. I tread carefully. "Okay, I'm supposed to say *yay*, right? He's giving you an office with your own window and everything?"

"Yes." Abby laughs a little, but that dies away quickly. "The window—it's very important." She meets my eyes, trepidation in hers. "The trouble is, that window, and the job, is in Los Angeles. I'm supposed to start on Wednesday."

Chapter Eleven

Abby

ZACH GOES SO VERY STILL that I wonder if he's breathing. His chest barely rises and falls.

What I want is to go into his arms, hold him. Tell him I don't want this to end—whatever this is. But a long-distance relationship? It works for some. That is, if both parties really and truly want the relationship to work, and if the separation is relatively short.

Zach has a great life here, is part of his family's company, and is immersed in charity work, which he loves—I can hear it in his voice when he talks about it. I want to ask him to come to L.A. with me, but that would mean Zach leaving his home and all he cares about.

He clears his throat. "Los Angeles. I thought you didn't want to move far from your mom."

"I don't. But she's married and settled, happy. And L.A. is only an hour flight away."

"That's true."

Zach has his hands on my arms, his fingers light. I fight to keep tears from my eyes. "So what do you think?" I ask shakily.

Zach stares at me so hard, I want to take a step back. Or hug him. Not sure which. A lump squeezes my throat.

"I think it's wonderful for you," Zach finally says. "Brent knows talent when he sees it. You deserve it."

A nice, supportive thing to say. But my spirits plummet. He's not begging me to stay. Or asking to come with me. Or blurting out, *But what about us?*

Maybe there is no *us*. A one-night-stand after a wedding, followed by an unexpected hook-up and a lot of phone calls. We've gotten to know each other well during those phone calls, probably better than if we'd talked in person. If we'd been in the same room, we'd have ended up in bed, not much talking happening.

I have to be realistic. We've begun a relationship, but it might be over before it gets off the ground. Sometimes that happens.

I'm sorry, I want to say, but I'm not sure Zach wants to hear it. I have no idea if what we have is as important to him as it is to me.

Zach's being very quiet again, his touch on my arms distracted, as though he's thinking of something else.

What do I expect? The great new job is about me, not him. I'll move on, and that will be it. The last time I moved away from Zach, it was many years before I saw him again. The lump in my throat grows.

"Zach?" If we're going to break up, I'd like him to pay attention.

Zach takes a breath and squeezes my arms before he releases me. "Abby. I have to ... Give me a minute to process this. Okay?"

"Okay."

And he turns around and walks out of the room. Just like that. No good-bye, no explanation, no telling me to enjoy the party before I go. He simply departs, fast, his footsteps echoing on the tile floor.

I squeeze my eyes shut as tears leak from them. Here I am, in Zach's house, a beautiful place, full of Zach's family and friends, and I'm alone.

————

I MAKE MYSELF NOT LEAVE THE PARTY, NO MATTER what Zach decides to do. This is for Calandra, welcoming her home. The least I can do is be happy for her.

Calandra gives me a severe eye as I return to the throng outside, but I shake my head. She's deep in relatives so she can't come to me. I take a glass of wine from Ben, who's handing them out at the bar set up by the pool, and drink a long gulp. Ben gives me a puzzled look but says nothing.

I notice Erin standing a little apart, as though she's not sure she should be here. I introduce myself and talk to her, because I'm feeling the same way. I like her as we start conversing—I ask her about ballet because I don't know much regarding it, and she speaks animatedly. Ben glances over at us a lot—I mean, a lot. If Erin notices, she makes no sign.

Soon it's time for the meal. We have it inside, in an echoing dining room with a long table. I can imagine it with the four McLaughlin brothers years and years ago —it must have been noisy and lively.

They're all here, the brothers, Calandra, the aunts and uncles, and Erin, greeted by Calandra, who pats the seat beside her. Ben quickly sits across from Erin, again unable to look at much else but her.

The crowd is chaotic as they surge around the table. There's no assigned seats. Everyone's grabbing a chair. They're going fast, and I fear I'll be next to Zach. I also fear I *won't* be next to him.

Suddenly, it's too much for me. I can't face a long, happy meal with people asking me questions. Has Zach or Calandra told anyone about my new job? Will I have to be radiant and excited?

I can't do it. I'll have to call Mrs. McLaughlin and apologize. Calandra will yell at me later, but I'll deal with that then.

I quietly slip out of the dining room, walking nonchalantly down the hall. Maybe the other guests will think I'm looking for the bathroom.

Stepping out the open back door, I make for the gate. On the other side is my SUV, and the way to my new life. The tears return, turning the house and yard into a blur of brick, green, and the brilliant scarlet of bougainvillea.

A woman steps in front of me. She's on the small side with gray hair and the McLaughlin blue eyes. Great Aunt Mary.

"Hello," I say awkwardly. "I was just ... um."

"Leaving." Great Aunt Mary pronounces the word firmly. "I'm here to see that you don't."

I blink. "Oh. Why?"

"Zach asked me to. He said you might try to go, and would I please look out and make sure you wait?"

"Oh." I can't think of another thing to say.

Great Aunt Mary slips her arm through mine. "You two are going through a difficult time, I can tell. It's always hard at first—you don't know what will happen, and you're scared of pain."

I let out a breath. "Exactly."

"It's much easier to stop everything before the pain happens." She speaks quietly but leads me back toward the house with surprising strength. "But then you'll never know if the good things will happen too. I was married fifty-three years. Every one of them worth it."

I have nothing to answer to that. Some marriages do work out, stretching into decades of contentedness. I think Calandra and Ryan have that chance—I remember telling her that.

It's different, I want to argue, but I remain silent. I'm at a crossroads, one thrust upon me. Three and a half weeks ago, I hadn't run into Zach and I hadn't known Brent would contact me. My life had run along on its usual tracks, no deviations. Now everything was about to change.

Great Aunt Mary takes me back into the dining room. No one has noticed me going, as they're all still settling themselves at the table. Great Aunt Mary motions to two places at the table's corner.

"Sit here with me, dear."

It's a command. I sit.

The lunch / early dinner is family style. Platters and bowls of food are passed around, and we all help ourselves. I take little, but Great Aunt Mary slops plenty onto her plate.

"You don't have enough of these tamales, honey." She plops two small corn-husk wrapped, wonderful-smelling tamales in front of me. "Alan spent all day making and steaming these. His tamales are to die for."

Alan is Mr. McLaughlin. I allow the tamales to stay.

Virginia McLaughlin stands up next to Alan at the head of the table. She tinks a knife to her glass until she has our attention.

"Before we start, I want us all to raise a toast to Calandra and Ryan. Our two kids home again, ready to begin life."

"To Calandra and Ryan!" I join in the salute, so glad for Calandra. She deserves all the happiness she's achieved.

I expect Virginia to have Ryan make a speech, but she only gives Calandra a kiss on the cheek and sits down. Everyone takes a sip of wine or beer or iced tea or water and prepares to attack the food.

"Hang on." Now Zach is on his feet, next to Ryan. "I have something I want to say."

The conversations that have started up fade again. I assume Zach will congratulate his brother and new sister, as he had at the wedding, maybe try out a few jokes.

Zach clears his throat. "The last time I got up and made a toast, a very wise woman told me to go with what was in my heart."

He swings his gaze to me, his blue eyes penetrating.

Now everyone's staring at *me*, but I see only Zach. I shakily lift my wine glass to him.

"So I'm speaking from the heart," Zach continues. The room quiets down, the family and guests listening with interest. "I lost track of Abby Warren a long time ago, when she moved out of my life. We were kids then, but I was happy to have the chance to reconnect with her, glad that Calandra and Ryan brought her back to me. Now she tells me she might have to move again, even farther away this time."

A series of sad *ohs,* fill the room. Zach's family, except for Calandra, look at me in surprise. Great Aunt Mary pats my hand.

"She's been offered a terrific job, a good opportunity for her, so I understand why she wants to go. But Abby also gave me *great* advice when she told me to speak from the heart." Zach fixes me with his gaze once more. "My heart says that I don't want to lose her again."

My pulse starts to throb, faster, faster. I'm burning inside, scared and hopeful at the same time.

"I've been talking it over with Mom and Dad, and they've decided it's a great idea. So I'm going to make a counteroffer to you, Abby. A job at McLaughlin Renovations, doing our marketing and ad sales—help we truly need. No more Austin on the side of a bus."

Everyone bursts out laughing, including Austin. "Aw, come on," Austin shouts. "My one chance at fame."

Zach watches me without smiling as he waits for the laughter to die down. "The salary is not as high probably, but you'll save on airfare visiting your mom. Plus, you'll get a window. I know that's important to you."

Zach stops, as though he's run out of words.

I sit with my mouth open. Stunned. Zach offering me what I want—a job in my hometown with freedom from Mr. Beale. No more personality-less cubicles. I'd have the warm friendliness I see between the McLaughlins, and I won't have to move out of state, or even out of the Phoenix area.

Virginia nods at me. "We decided this even before you told Zach about your job offer in California. He's right—we need someone like you. Besides, if you leave town, he'll be impossible to live with."

Laughter ripples. The whole room watches me, avid, waiting for my answer. Ben, Austin, and Ryan are grinning at me, encouraging. They don't look at all unhappy that Zach wants me on board.

I'm put on the spot, but on the other hand, Zach is handing me something wonderful.

"But wait, there's more." Zach sets down his bottle of beer. "Hold off on that decision, Abby, until you hear my next question."

He leaves his place and walks down the table to me, scooting around the guests until he's standing next to me.

Then he goes down on one knee. He takes out a little velvet box, which he opens to reveal a ring with a lovely diamond glittering against white satin.

"Abby Warren," he says, studying me with fine blue eyes that have gazed down at me in the night. "Will you marry me?"

Now the room holds its breath. I do too. If I breathe, I'll start hyperventilating or something, making a serious fool of myself.

Zach's brow puckers as the silence stretches. "Just to be clear—the job offer isn't contingent on this. You'll mostly be working with my mom anyway, and you can telecommute if you want. You never even have to see me."

He smooths out his face, his gorgeous face, and gazes at me alone. The room and the guests fade. As when we'd danced at the wedding reception, it's Zach and me, by ourselves, the rest of the world inconsequential. I know he's speaking directly from his heart —to mine.

"I love you, Abs," he whispers. "Whether you stay or go, whether you say yes or no, I love you. I gotta be honest and tell you that."

"Well, that's good," I whisper back. "Because I love *you*."

Great Aunt Mary bounces in her seat. "Was that a yes? You'll have to speak up. I'm hard of hearing."

"No, you aren't," Zach tells her, and at the same time I say, very loudly: "Yes!"

The room erupts in noise. At the end of the table, Calandra is on her feet, yelling her joy. Ryan hugs her. Zach's mom is crying, wiping her eyes with a napkin. Alan puts his arm around her, wearing the biggest smile I've ever seen.

Great Aunt Mary gives me a squashing hug, eyes brimming, smile wide. Austin and Ben whoop and high-five each other. Erin laughs in excitement and Ben's laughter dies when Erin beams across the table at him.

Zach ... Zach is still on one knee, holding out the ring. I take the ring, place it on the table, then stand up, pulling him up with me.

Then I kiss him.

I mash my face against his, lips to lips, as we'd done at age thirteen when we'd kissed for the first time. Zach understands and laughs as we part, throwing back his head, his laughter warm and comforting.

He gathers me to him and our mouths meet in a much better kiss. It's one that goes on and on as everyone cheers and hoots.

If I'd known way back then, when I'd first dared myself to kiss Zach McLaughlin, that I'd have my arms around him today, he fulfilling my wildest dreams, I wouldn't have troubled myself with unhappiness.

The loneliness wouldn't have mattered. I'd have known that Zach would be waiting for me at the end of the dark tunnel.

Known he'd put his arms around me, smile, kiss me ... and change everything.

Epilogue

Zach

"I DIDN'T PLAN it this way," I say to Abby two weeks later.

We're strolling alone by the pool in my folks' backyard, the night cool after a hot day. Oleanders are blooming, anticipating summer. We're back at the family homestead, a smaller gathering this time, to celebrate our engagement.

"I was supposed to take you to a fancy restaurant, get you liquored up with wine and single malt, and then spring the proposal on you."

"This was better." Abby slides her hand to mine, locking fingers with me. "In front of your whole family. More fun than with strangers."

"More embarrassing for me if you'd said no." I tighten our hand-clasp. "Strangers would sympathize, but my family would never let it go. They'd critique. Hold up cards with numbers to show how I did."

Abby laughs, bumping into me. "Your family is great."

My brothers aren't bad, I agree, when they decide to be decent guys. Right now they're talking to Abby's mom and her new husband. I remember Abby's mom from when we were kids, a dynamic woman with a big smile. She and Abby are much alike.

Calandra is hiking across the yard toward us, dragging Ryan behind her. He doesn't look all that unhappy about being pulled around by his wife. The macho big brother who never needed anybody has been felled by love.

Calandra plants herself in front of us, her face lit by the spotlights around the pool. "Hi. I won the argument. You get to be the first to know."

"I didn't argue that hard," Ryan says. "But you get to explain it to Mom."

Calandra's broad smile holds excitement. "We're going to have a baby."

Abby drops my hand. She squeals. She rushes at Calandra and they hug, clinging hard to each other. Ryan's eyes are misty as he watches Calandra.

I grab Ryan's hand and pump his arm up and down. "Congratulations, bro. That didn't take long."

"We were going to wait, but, um, well ..." Ryan goes about three shades of red, and I bust up laughing.

"I always knew you couldn't keep it in your pants."

I clap Ryan on the shoulder then pull him into a bear hug. "Seriously, dude, that's awesome. I get to be an uncle."

I'm making fun of Ryan, but it's not like Abby and I have kept away from each other. She's slept at my house, or I've stayed at her apartment, and we aren't watching television, trust me. My bed has a new hollow in the middle, but it fits us just fine.

Abby's moving in with me at the end of next week and will start at McLaughlin Renovations as soon as she's settled into my house. Means I get to wake up with her every morning, have breakfast—probably after more sex—head into the office ... I'm looking forward to it.

Abby and Calandra finally let each other go, wiping their eyes.

"I wanted to tell you first, not just because Abby's my best friend," Calandra says. "But so you two can slip away and be alone, like I know you're jonesing to."

Now Abby is several shades of red. "No way—this party is for us. And my mom's here."

"And we're about to upstage you. So go on. Enjoy it." Calandra flutters her fingers at Abby as though she's bestowing a gift.

Calandra and Ryan walk away, hand in hand, ready to spring their news on the unsuspecting family. Ryan nearly bounces across the lawn. I've never seen the man so happy.

"She's trying to make up for the fact that she and

Ryan didn't spend their engagement having sex," Abby says. "Well, not the *entire* engagement. They were hitting it plenty whenever they were speaking to each other."

"Yeah, I remember the drama. The ups, the downs. Like a storm that moves where you don't expect."

"To be fair, Ryan could be a pain in the ass sometimes. No offense," Abby adds quickly.

"None taken. You're right." I watch my brother pull Calandra close as they approach my parents and hers. "He drove me bat-crap crazy. We're not like *them*." I slide my arm around Abby's waist, let my hand drift downward. "We're a perfect couple."

Abby slants me a look from her sexy eyes. "Sure about that?"

"Yep. We're in love, we have sex every time we can ... Calandra's nice to give us the opportunity. All the waiting is ... tense."

Her smile lights her face. "You mean once we marry, we'll have sex every night?"

"That's my plan." I take in her mirth and flush. "I mean, if it's your plan too. I'm not an asshole."

Abby snakes her fingers around the lapels of my shirt and pulls me to her. "I plan to have my wicked way with you, whenever and however often I can. You okay with that?"

Instead of waiting for an answer, she plants a long kiss on my mouth, one that has me hot and wanting in no time flat.

"It's a five minute drive to my house," I murmur.

"I know."

I kiss Abby on the mouth again, she tasting like sugar and everything nice.

Across the yard, my mom and Calandra's erupt into screeches of joy. My dad, always quiet, bestows on them a big smile. Austin lets out a whoop that can be heard the length and breadth of the neighborhood. Ben flashes an excited smile. He draws near Erin, who was also invited, but halts a few steps from of her, as though there's a barrier between them.

Abby squeezes my hand. "Calandra's right. We've been upstaged. I say we go."

"Sounds good."

We flee. No one notices but Ben as Abby and I sneak off like teenagers, jump in my truck and glide away, laughing together.

We make it home without anyone texting or calling and reaming us out. We're up the stairs and to my room —our room now—moonlight pouring in and turning the air silver.

Abby's body is gorgeous as she strips, she undulating in a little dance, like we'd done on our first one-night stand. I catch her, her skin warm, and press kisses all over her.

In no time at all, we're on the bed, me inside her, she touching my face and making soft sounds of pleasure. Both of our voices rise in volume as we make love as hard as we can, the cool moonlight sliding over us.

Abby's eyes are soft, her smile all for me. This

woman came back into my life and healed it, and this time, I'm never letting her go.

———

Ben

I'M THE ONLY ONE WHO SEES ABBY AND ZACH RUN off into the night. I'm glad for my brother—the grouchy shit has found some happiness at last.

I'm glad for Ryan too—his announcement that he's going to be a dad has turned the party into a huge celebration.

Erin is excited for them, bouncing on her toes. She moves with grace no matter what she does. She clicks a mouse with a precision that's like music, and I could watch her sort mail all day.

I am so screwed.

Erin's a temp, and I know one day she'll go. She loves dancing, and she'll let nothing keep her from it. She'll say good-bye, and the agency will send another secretary, and that will be that.

So, I'm going to enjoy being near her as long as I can. Maybe I'll drum up the courage to ask her out. Maybe. She'll turn me down probably, but hey, a geek has to try.

And I will.

One day.

The family cheers again, and Erin looks over at me,

flashing me her warm smile, her eyes lighting up behind her glasses.

Like I said ... screwed.

———

THANK YOU FOR READING! DON'T MISS *WHY Don't You Stay ... Forever?* Ben and Erin's story, Book 2 in the McLaughlin Brothers series.

Primal Bonds

Bodyguard

Wild Cat

Hard Mated

Mate Claimed

"Perfect Mate" (novella)

Lone Wolf

Tiger Magic

Feral Heat

Wild Wolf

Bear Attraction

Mate Bond

Lion Eyes

Bad Wolf

Wild Things

White Tiger

Guardian's Mate

Red Wolf

Midnight Wolf

Tiger Striped

A Shifter Christmas Carol

Iron Master

Shifter Made ("Prequel" short story)

About the Author

New York Times bestselling and award-winning author Jennifer Ashley has written more than 100 published novels and novellas in romance, urban fantasy, mystery, and historical fiction under the names Jennifer Ashley, Allyson James, and Ashley Gardner. Jennifer's books have been translated into more than a dozen languages and have earned starred reviews in *Publisher's Weekly* and *Booklist*. When she isn't writing, Jennifer enjoys playing music (guitar, piano, flute), reading, hiking, and building dollhouse miniatures.

More about Jennifer's books can be found at
http://www.jenniferashley.com

To keep up to date on her new releases, join her newsletter here:

http://eepurl.com/47kLL

38   86

Made in the USA
Columbia, SC
15 June 2020

10841579R00088